WORD OF MOUTH

WORD OF MOUTH

M.A.C. FARRANT

Thistledown Press Ltd.

© M.A.C. Farrant, 1996
All rights reserved

Canadian Cataloguing in Publication Data

Farrant, M.A.C. (Marion Alice Coburn)

Word of mouth

ISBN 1-895449-60-X

I. Title.

PS8561.A76W67 1996   C813'.54   C96-920053-6
PR199.3.F37W67 1996

Book design by A.M. Forrie
Set in Caslon 540
by Thistledown Press

Printed and bound in Canada
by Veilleux Printing
Boucherville, Quebec

Thistledown Press Ltd.
633 Main Street
Saskatoon, Saskatchewan, S7H 0J8

Thistledown Press acknowledges the support received for its publishing program from the Saskatchewan Arts Board and the Canada Council's Block Grants program.

ACKNOWLEDGEMENTS

Versions or excerpts of these stories appeared in the following magazines: "Refusal" in *Writ 27*, 1995; "The Real Story" as "The Best Time" in the *Toronto Star*, 1994; and "Secrets" in *Minus Tides*, 1996.

Special thanks to Susan Musgrave for editorial advice and to Terry Farrant for love and everything else.

The support of the cultural Services Branch, B.C. Ministry of Small Business, Tourism, and Culture and the Canada Council is gratefully acknowledged.

For Elsie
Doreen and Shirley

and in memory of my father
Capt. W.D. Gibson

CONTENTS

Part I   Sybilla

THE REAL STORY   13

HUMAN NATURE   25

KEEP THIS AND NEVER LOSE IT   51

Part II   Word of Mouth

REFUSAL   65

SECRETS   83

NAVIGATION   111

*. . . word of mouth is sound made in the echo of God . . . ear to mouth,
mouth to ear, it soon became the people's knowledge.*

— Grace Paley
"Later The Same Day"

Part 1

Sybilla

THE REAL STORY

People are always asking about my mother. If it's a worker of some sort, I tell them to get lost, take a hike, get off my back. If they're really on my case, trying to squeeze some old dead feelings out of me then I'm likely to go strange on them. "You want feelings," I tell them, "well, how about these?" And I'll throw a twister, yell and swear. I'm nineteen now, they don't got a right to be asking more questions.

But fact is, I don't remember much about my mother. And what I do remember ain't that great. I was eight when they took me away for good. Eight and a half when she died drunk, choking on her own vomit in the Craigmyle Motel. She was twenty-seven.

Mostly what I remember is being locked in rooms with a bag of chips and a pop and watching TV. I guess they were motel rooms. Just a couple of beds, a TV, and the curtains drawn. There was this one place we had to climb steps to. An apartment maybe. I remember eating fish and chips at a table with my mother and some guy. There was always some guy. But only one kid — me — that I know of.

My mother had long blonde hair, probably dyed. This is the main thing I remember about how she looked. Which is why I dye mine, I guess, though mine's cut short. And she was always dressing up in skirts and jewellery. Looked like someone on TV selling shampoo. I don't remember if she had a job. But she wasn't a hooker, I'm sure of that. Don't even suggest it. She was probably on welfare. Like me.

She drank, though, which is what did her in. Half the time she never knew I was around. She'd be sleeping the day away so I'd sneak out. Maybe I was six or seven. Go in her purse then find a store. I was addicted to candy. The little candies for a dime or a quarter — candy bananas and strawberries, packs of licking powder, *Nerds, Dubble Bubble.*

When she found out she'd smack me. Start hollering about the money, about how useless I was, nothing but a thief. But I'd just stand there. I wouldn't cry. I don't ever remember crying back then. I didn't start crying till I had Christian, the first kid, and now I think I'll never stop.

But the crying's not about Rita, my mother. It's about me being a single mom. How I'm only nineteen got two little kids already. About how I'm wrecked half the time from being up with one of them sick. How I never gets enough money from welfare to feed my animals, my beautiful cats and dogs. How everything's so hard.

There's other girls my age having different kinds of lives and no kids dragging after them. I sees them at the mall, whole bunches of them hanging around the perfume counter in Eatons. Why couldn't that be me?

◆◆◆

When was I took away? It's not clear in my head. I think there was a bunch of people — cops, social workers for sure. I think it was night but that's hard to tell cause the curtains was always closed. First I went to some house for a couple of weeks, then to Alderwood. *Alderwood Treatment Centre For Emotionally Disturbed Children* is the whole horrible name.

But there was lots of food there. And TV. And I started school, never having been before. But I didn't figure I'd be there for good, like five years. I didn't figure Rita would be history, that I'd never see her again. I always thought I'd go back to some motel room and there she'd be sleeping in the other bed. And me, I'd be on the floor eating candy, watching TV. Being left alone. With no one bugging me.

◆◆◆

The bugging started at Alderwood. And it never quit. If it wasn't other kids swiping your stuff or pushing you around it was workers yapping on about feelings. They used to think it was good if you got mad. So they was always at you. "How do you feel, Sybilla?" They'd be saying this till you'd wanna punch them. And when you finally did start hitting they'd wrestle you to the ground and sit on you saying, "That's good, Sybilla, let it all out, Sybilla, tell us how you really feel." Always figuring I had these deep feelings about my mother. But I didn't. Only about them and how I hated them always at me, pretending they cared when, really, they was getting paid to look after us.

At Alderwood there was three houses: Alder House, Cedar House and Birch House — that was my house, we called it Bitch House. There was six workers to a house, plus two supervisors. And the week was divided in half. For years I thought regular families lived like that — Sunday to Wednesday, Wednesday to Saturday. A bunch of adults looking after the kids, eight kids to a house. With workers taking turns sleeping over in the staff room. With big meetings around the dining room table every Wednesday afternoon, talking about the kids and how bad they'd been.

While I was there I had different kids sharing my room in the girl's wing. Kathy who'd spend whole days in her pyjamas laying on the bed holding a teddy bear, staring at nothing. And weird Barbara with her bugs, her pet spiders and flies she kept in boxes and let crawl on her. She was the first one I ran away with. We stole a worker's Volkswagen, rolled it down the hill into a ditch. And then there was Cindy, an Indian. Two hundred pounds already when she was twelve, in for B&E's. Cindy was the best thing that ever happened to me at Alderwood.

So mostly I'm pissed off about my mother. It's her fault I got put in Alderwood and it's her fault for the way I'm living now. And my dad? All I know is Rita saying this: "The whole world's full of assholes called Rob and your dad's one of them."

◆◆◆

I try all the time not to think about Alderwood. But it's hard. Everything reminds me of being there. Like Halloween last night. This morning there's smashed pumpkins all over the street, some of them hollowed out with faces, all broken up and only a stupid smile showing or one eye. It's been raining hard and cars have been driving through them so there's mushy yellow stuff on the road with tire tracks going through it.

Christian and me did a pumpkin, made a scary face and put a candle inside. But I kept it in the house knowing it'd get wrecked by the gangs of kids roaming around. Not that they'd come to this welfare dump — through all the mud in the yard and up the broken steps. It's a crime the places we gotta live.

I took Christian and the baby to a couple of houses up the street. He was Spiderman, his most favourite guy. The baby, she was nothing. And me, I puts on an old dog mask we had around the house and this makes Christian and the baby laugh.

So I'm thinking about Alderwood again and the Halloweens we used to have there. They'd let us be anything we wanted on Halloween saying it was good therapy or some such shit. So we'd all be gangsters, or murderers, or pirates. And once Alan Kamouroski was a serial killer dressed up in an old raincoat and a baseball cap, and a rope around his waist for tying up people. I guess you'd say we was having fun.

❖ ❖ ❖

Let me tell you about the best time I ever had, the Halloween me and Cindy decided we was gonna dress up as hookers. There was this big staff meeting about would it be okay and we was called in and told to say our feelings about why we wanted to do this. We must of made up something good cause they let us. Mostly we wanted to wear piles of make-up. So they had to take us to Shopper's Drug Mart and buy us some.

But before we can dress up this night we gotta have supper. And it's torture. There we are, all sitting around the big dining room table eating pork chops and mashed potatoes. Eight kids and three workers. We'd only just started when two of the younger boys has to sit away from the table for throwing food, they was so excited. This is what they did to you if you was bad at the table, made you sit out.

But this night it didn't calm things down like it was supposed to cause right after the boys sits back Barbara starts drooling mashed potatoes out of her mouth thinking it's funny, saying, "Watch me pop my pimples." And so everyone has to try doing this and gets yelled at. Pretty soon there's strings of mashed potatoes all over the table looking like white worms. So things are starting to get wild. With everyone grabbing food and banging each other with their elbows and flinging bits of potato around.

Then Davey, this idiot-stick, starts shaking the ketchup bottle with the lid off and it goes all over a worker's head. Carlos, who's sitting next to him. And then the shift leader, Judy, starts screaming at him from the end of the table saying, "How dare you spoil our meal," and, "Go take your chair and sit against the wall." But he don't. He gets all mad and stands up grabbing the table like he's gonna flip it over. Carlos has to jump him, drag him out to the hall kicking and screaming. He's got ketchup all over his head and shirt and now some of it's on Davey who suddenly thinks it's blood and starts shrieking about that. We can hear him from out in the hall yelling: "It was an accident, God, it was an accident, leave me alone, you're breaking my arm, get this blood off me, you're killing me, help, help, this hormone's killing me."

With everything so wild me and Cindy starts knocking over glasses of milk saying, "Whoops sorry." And then Cindy starts farting real loud, she was good at that, and one of the smaller boys falls off his chair saying he's been poisoned and then Kathy for no reason starts biting her own arm and making these weird noises like an owl going, "Hoot, hoot, hoot," loud as she can.

I grabs this worker's smokes and shoves one in my mouth and she's trying to grab it back saying, "Sybilla, you're really pushing it this time, you're going to miss Halloween if you keep this up." But I manages to stuff the package and the matches in my jeans and run like hell into the kitchen with the worker right after me like we was playing tag. Pretty soon all the kids are off their chairs and racing around too. And only three workers and one of them's on top of Davey out in the hall. And he's still screaming, "Help, I'm being murdered."

I gives Alan Kamouroski the matches. He's in Alderwood for burning down a school so this makes him happy and he starts a fire in the kitchen out of paper napkins and it's burning real good when a bunch of workers from the other houses comes charging in and one of them's got a fire extinguisher spraying foam all over the cupboard where it's burning. I guess Judy must of phoned them. But not before everyone's gone in the fridge and got out the tub of margarine and starts smearing it over each other and on the walls and then it gets on the floor so there's workers and kids slipping and falling and Davey's still screaming from the hall and Kathy's still hooting like an owl, the only one left at the table.

Cindy decides to go help Davey and runs and jumps on Carlos' back but don't get to hurt him cause we hear the fire truck with its siren coming up the driveway and everyone races outside to see where the fire is. And watch the firemen pull the thick grey hoses into the house yelling at us all serious, "Stand back, outta the way." They has on yellow jackets and boots bringing all kinds of mud in the house. In the kitchen a couple of them slips in the margarine.

But this slows things down long enough for the workers to get in charge again. And when the firemen finally leaves there's this crisis meeting in the living room. With all the kids getting a supreme therapy session layed on them. With the workers saying how they're so disappointed in our behaviour and wondering now if we should be allowed to go trick or treating at all because of the way we acted. It went on forever till it was too late to go anywheres. So all we do is go to the Alderwood bonfire down by the tool shed and watch some useless fireworks.

After we're in bed that night the workers have another meeting in the staff room. One of the big supervisors comes in especially. Cindy and me sneaks down the hall and try to listen at the door. Mostly we can hear Judy, the shift leader, getting in trouble. About losing control. We can hear her crying in there.

And a girl worker saying, "That's all right Judy, let it all out, tell us how you feel."

◆◆◆

Feelings. Nothing but feelings. That's what Alderwood was. So big deal. I learned about feelings. You think it does me any good now? Get real. This is Sybilla talking. Listen to this. Every time I asks welfare how come we gotta live in shit box houses or crummy apartments, every time I TELL THEM MY FEELINGS, they always says this: "That's all that's available Sybilla." Shrugging me off. Like really. You should see the place we're in now. A cheap rental dump that's gonna be torn down for townhouses. When? I don't know. But it's the only dump around here I'll tell you that much.

It's unreal. Like coming down this dead end street . . . the wide road, sidewalks, trees every so often, big trees that drop their leaves in the fall. And all these jazzed up houses with their huge lawns and flower beds, with their new cars and their boats parked in the driveways. Some of the houses look just like them places you see on TV. Big white houses with all their lights on at night and inside there's Mom and Dad and a bunch of sucky blonde kids.

Then you come to the end of the street and the nightmare we're in. It's a mystery how it got here. I mean it's your basic poverty job. Sometimes I figure it was just dropped here. Like by helicopter. Welfare playing another sick joke on people like me. Saying, "Here, you can live where all the rich people live but you can't be one of them." Because there's nothing like this house for miles around. A shack is what it is, made of wood shingles that're always falling off. Front porch steps made of broken boards. A roof that leaks in winter right onto the kitchen floor. The yard full of weeds and long grass. Something you'd see an old weird person living in, some strange old guy living stinking and miserable all by himself.

Whenever I complain I gets shot down. "Be thankful you're not on the street, Sybilla," is what welfare says.

◆◆◆

So now my problem's being on welfare and living in dumps, eh? Back then it was living with crazies. Like at the Danforth Street group home. Where I went after Alderwood, when I was thirteen.

The guy who ran the place lived there all the time. Robert. He had his son living there too, Hayden, a brain-damaged guy, maybe sixteen, always playing this acid rock really loud. Always walking around with a hard on, trying to get the girls to screw him. A small weasel guy.

"Wanna do it?" he'd be slobbering, any time he could get you alone.

And I'd go, "Like don't make me puke, Hayden, I'd rather screw a rat."

There was another crazy living there too, a real head case, Lindsay Wilson. This kid was so messed up he had a worker with him all the time, day and night. He was always breaking things, trying to hurt himself, screaming over nothing stuff like not wanting what he was having for lunch.

He was a fat guy, thirteen or fourteen, with a giant head and long black hair. When he started wrecking his furniture they took all his stuff away. Everything. The bed, the dresser, even his comics. One time he got so mad after they'd done this he started tearing up the walls making huge holes with only his hands and feet. Pulled the cupboard doors off their hinges, pulled the boards off the window. Then he smashed the window and took off. But didn't go anywhere. That was the crazy part. All he did was run down the road then come back. Start hucking rocks through the living room window, yelling from outside.

The workers caught him no problem. He hardly fought back. Pretty soon he's in his room again being made to clean up the mess, help fix the walls and window. And for a couple of weeks things are okay, no more fits. So he gets his furniture back, gets to be in the house with the rest of us. But it don't last long. He has a spaz one night about cookies, wanting more, and starts throwing knives and forks at everyone. And he's locked in his room again.

So there we are this time sitting around the lunch table. Me, Robert, Hayden, the other kids. And we can hear Lindsay yelling from down the hall. Then we hears a crash like he's thrown his chair against the door. Robert says to himself, "Time to take out the furniture." But don't move and goes on eating.

Hayden starts laughing this phoney laugh, acting Mr. Big Guy like he's some kind of worker, and points down the hall saying, "Maybe we oughta take his clothes off him, see how he likes it with his balls hanging out." And goes to grab his dad's cigarettes.

But Robert grabs the smokes and moves them out of Hayden's way. "Buy your own cigarettes," he says, "you got an allowance," and this pisses Hayden off — it didn't take much — and he starts screaming at Robert: "You asshole, you just wait, you're gonna get it."

◆◆◆

That Christmas Robert has a party. With all kinds of food — cakes, chips, cheesies, pop, pizza. And invites the relatives of the kids living there. Guess who comes for me? A child care worker I never seen before, Bonnie. But brings me a present, a Sony Walkman, which is okay because it's got headphones and I won't have to listen to Hayden's music no more.

Lindsay's mother comes to the party, too. I couldn't believe it. Drives up in this hot car, a rich broad. You couldn't figure how she'd have such a nut case for a kid. At the party, Lindsay spends all his time sitting on the couch beside her acting stupid, showing off. Like stuffing his face with cake and seeing how far he can spit out the crumbs. Getting her food and banging into the coffee table, knocking everything on the floor. Breaking a couple of glasses with pop in them. Tripping Hayden when he goes by, that was okay. But this mother don't do dick about it, just ignores Lindsay, talking to the other adults about her real estate business, eating her Christmas cake off of the paper plate, smiling. And she don't stay longer than an hour. Says, "Good-bye sweetie," to Lindsay who's whining at the front door, who's begging in this high squeaky voice, "Oh please Mom, don't go, I gotta show you my baseball cards." "Some other time," she says, patting his arm. After she's gone Lindsay goes strange. In front of everyone. Shoves his head into the fridge handle and cuts it so bad Robert has to get an ambulance. After that Lindsay goes to the nut house for good.

◆ ◆ ◆

In January I decides I won't go to public school no more. There I was nearly fouteen in Grade 4. Get serious. No way was I gonna be in a class with a bunch of little kids. So I had to do this correspondence at the kitchen table all morning, every morning. But the stuff I had to do was so dumb — learning about old wars, reading stories about animals that could talk and go on adventures. Like duh. And math! Gimme a break. I couldn't figure it out. So I says to Robert, "I'm not doing this shit, it's stupid." And he'd say, "You'll be stupid if you don't do it." Then I'd say, "Screw you." Then he'd say, "All right then, no TV till you do your work." And on it went.

Not long after that I ran away. Took some money I seen Robert put in a drawer plus all of Hayden's acid rock tapes. And threw them in a ditch. It was raining hard that day so I knew they'd get wrecked.

◆ ◆ ◆

Let me tell you something else. One more thing. There's a filing cabinet down at welfare stuffed full of papers about me. Piles and piles of papers going back years and years. About the places I've lived and everything that's happened to me. Reports, assessments, every kind of test. All these people having meetings about me, writing things down. You think these papers tell the real story about Sybilla? Don't make me laugh. The real story's the one I'm telling right now. The one that never gets told.

HUMAN NATURE

This always happens: you sits down talk to a stranger and pretty soon they starts telling you this, they say: "My life, what a story, I could write a book about it." And then you gets to hear some boring stuff about people dying and the hard times they've had, or about some asshole who walked out on them or, if it's a guy, the time some woman screwed him over. All kinds of stories. Don't matter if they're young or old. But if they're old it's always about how no one visits them, especially their grown-up kids. How the only times they sees them is at Christmas, Mother's day, their birthdays. If they're lucky.

Like Mrs. Harrison next door. Always moaning about her old bones, how they're hurting all the time. How it's hard to get up in the morning make herself food. How she can never remember what day it is or where she's put her slippers or her glasses. "Sybilla," she says, "you don't know the half of it, you think you got it bad." And then she shakes her head, drinks her tea. Her white hair's so thin you can see her pink head.

First time I goes over there I gets the whole story. Two husbands both dead, neither one any good. A son sounding like a regular jerk-off, only coming round when he's wanting money, never paying it back. A daughter the other side of the country hardly visits hardly phones. And grandchildren she hates. "All they want is presents," Mrs. Harrison says, "and don't expect a thank you."

She's living on her pension in this big stone house that looks like a mansion. "Built before the war," she says. "War? What war?" I says, never remembering any war.

"The war, the war," she says getting all mad, waving her hand behind her.

Her place is run down, dark and smelly inside, the furniture a thousand years old, brown and worn out. Telling her story pretty soon her dry old eyes start crying. It's like she's bleeding sadness. As soon as she opens her mouth out comes a truck load of misery. To dump over me. And if she ain't bawling, she's complaining.

I hadn't known her a week when she's sucked me into going to the doctor's office with her. In her car that she hardly ever uses, keeps hidden in the garage. But she gets me to go because she says this: "I'm afraid I'll pass out Sybilla, I'm feeling so weak."

What a mark I am. So I says okay, thinking maybe she'll return the favour some time, look after my kids, Christian and the baby, give me a break.

What an afternoon that was. Her driving so low in the seat she can hardly see over the steering wheel. Going way too slow, like we was going to a funeral. And doing all this talking about some person called Marnie who's got lung cancer but's doing better now she's got her oxygen tank. Then at the doctor's office she suddenly gets ten times more crippled than she really is, needing help to get in the door, getting all wimpy with the nurse. I starts wondering how we was gonna get the car home. I never learned to drive so I wouldn't be much help.

After the doctor's office it gets worse. First we have to get her pills waiting forever at the drug store, the kids acting up, me getting totally bored. Then it's stopping at Safeway for food, another forever, pushing that cart around for her and me drooling over all the stuff she's grabbing — Sara Lee cakes, huge bags of chocolate marshmallow cookies, Dad's Oatmeal cookies, cans of spaghetti, two whole chickens. You should see the stuff we eat — like Kraft Dinner, soup, piles of white bread.

Then in the car on the way home it's more stories. One about a woman gets caught in the Bay Parkade elevator losing both legs and an arm. How this woman wakes up in the hospital screaming about the blood. Then a long story about a woman at Silver Threads having a brain tumour the size of a baseball, how they operated but it was too late.

"It always is," says Mrs. Harrison, her mouth all tight, her face gone blotchy. Shaking her half-bald head. "Life is grim," she says, "and just gets grimmer and grimmer."

After that I figures I might as well go home and shoot myself. One time I was over there having coffee and went in her fridge to get some milk. And there's this bottle of champagne on the bottom shelf. "Oh wow," I says, "when's the party?"

"I've had that bottle in the fridge for fifteen years," she says, "never had anything to celebrate."

"Jesus, Mrs. Harrison, that's the shits."

"Call me Ivy," she says.

◆ ◆ ◆

So I tries not to visit so often. Because she's always wanting me to do things. Like clean her windows, or get her bread and milk at the corner store. She's got this washer and dryer on her back porch, eh? So one time I asks if I could use them. I mean I'm doing all this stuff for her it's the least she could do. Then I wouldn't have to lug the kids and everything to the laundromat in town. But when I asks her about it she goes all queer, suspicious like I was stealing something from her. "Oh no," she says, "Molly wouldn't like that." "Molly?" I goes. Then remember that's her useless daughter in Winnipeg. "That's right," Ivy says, "Molly says I shouldn't get involved."

So for a while I figures she can rot over there. Go talk to the walls. Tell *them* her stories. But before long she's knocking on my door. Sets the dogs off barking. And her looking all crinkled and small on my front porch steps. Thin as a leaf she is and all veiny too. "Here," she says, giving me five bucks, "for the kiddies." And smiles this feeble smile like it was hurting her. Like it was causing her a bigger pain than all the pains her old bones ever gives her.

I could hardly hear what she was saying over the dog's noise. But I figures it out, I ain't a total idiot. She was feeling lonely, more miserable than usual. So I starts feeling sorry for her and walks her home. With her complaining about her bad back, saying she wouldn't be surprised if it broke in half.

But she's strange, weird in the head. Another time I goes over there and she's all excited. I thought maybe she'd won the lottery. But she says, "Wait till you hear this Sybilla," and drags me inside. There's actually happiness in her voice and she's laughing away, telling me this: "He's dead. He blames himself. It's his father. They were on a fox hunt and he showed up drunk. Randolph couldn't stop him from riding the horse, and he fell off, dead. I thought there'd never be an end to him. And now he's finally dead. What a relief. We can get on with the wedding. Nicole and Robert can finally get married. There's nothing standing in the way now."

It took me a whole week to figure it out. She was talking about *All My Children*.

❖ ❖ ❖

Here's another story. About the McHatties live the other side of us. She lives upstairs, he lives down. Separate kitchens and everything. When they ain't fighting each other they gang up on me. Like from day one. Picture this: knock, knock — there's this short fat pair standing on my porch. Dressed up like twins they are, black pants, brown jackets, except she's the one with the diamonds on every finger. He's the one with the bald head and teensy eyes so puffy you can hardly see his eyeballs. Got brown blotches on his hands and face and neck.

"Yeah?" I says.

She does all the talking, says, "I hope you keep your kids in the yard because we won't be responsible for them if they get out."

No hello, welcome to the neighbourhood, nice to meet you, what's your name? But wham, a load of crap. You don't need to hit me over the head to know they got it in for single mothers on welfare. So right away I hates them and I goes: "So who's asking ya to watch my kids?" I mean the baby couldn't even walk then.

"There's no need to get huffy, young lady," the bald McHattie goes. "We're just telling you. And we wouldn't appreciate any wild parties either. This is a quiet neighbourhood. There's families and decent people living here and we don't want to be kept up nights."

"What makes you think I'll be having wild parties?" I goes.

"Well," he goes.

And we stand there glaring at each other. Then Mrs. McHattie says, "We just wanted to let you know. We don't want any problems." And they takes off.

I slams the door. Mad as anything. Then phones up welfare. "What the hell are decent people?" I yells. "Can you answer me that?"

Welfare says, "Calm down Sybilla. You got to learn to get on with people. They just don't want any trouble."

"So why should there be trouble?"

Welfare says: "What about that incident last year? With you calling the police about your boyfriend?"

"I don't got a right to call the cops if the asshole's bothering me?"

Welfare goes, with this big pause ... "Sybilla."

"What?"

"Just behave yourself and everything will be all right."

Just behave yourself. Jesus. What did that ever get me?

◆ ◆ ◆

The McHatties. Claude and Margaret. I call them the McHates. Your so-called "decent people". One time I was passing their house going to the store with the kids and I seen a box of magazines at the end of their driveway. Full of *Playboy* and *Penthouse* and some hard core porn stuff with naked guys on the fronts. I knows cause I stops and has a look through the box. Never knowing what you'll find for free. And Margaret McHate starts screaming at me from the top window.

"Leave 'em alone. They're for garbage."

Naturally I ignores her. So pretty soon she's charging out the house in her bare feet and yellow dressing gown, yelling some more. "I said, leave 'em alone, they're filth."

"Yeah, I can see that," I says, "but I never figured you'd be reading this stuff Margaret." Having a laugh.

This gets her going. She gets all twisted. "They're not mine," she's shouting, "they're his," and jerks her head back towards the house where Claude McHate lives in the basement.

Coming back from the store I catches him from the end of the street. Picking up the box and hurrying back inside with it like he'd just stole something. Now I know why his eyes are so puffy. From all that reading. After that when I sees him I always says this: "Hey Claude, read any good books lately?" And laugh even if I don't feel like it. Just to see him squirm, the old pervert.

◆ ◆ ◆

I'd sure like to be a fly on their walls. To watch the fights. Late at night I hear them screaming. Her with this high, sharp voice, him with a loud, growly one. They makes so much noise I hears them when I'm laying in bed. One time an upstairs window got broke. Cr-aaash. A kitchen chair goes flying onto the front lawn. It was still laying there the next morning. Another time one of them gets in the car backing up so fast they smashes into a telephone pole. The whole back end of their new Honda's was wrecked. They're boozers. This is what I figure. A couple of mean drunks. Crazies.

Which is the story of *my* life. How there's always crazies. If I'm not living with them like I used to in group homes and the treatment centre, then they're living next to me like now: on the one side weird old Ivy, on the other, the McHates. Here's something: don't let anyone tell you all the crazies are poor people. I know for a fact what's true: crazies are everywhere. But especially in rich neighbourhoods like where I'm living now. This place is full of them. And they're different from the crazy people I'm used to seeing in all the crummy apartments I've ever lived. At least *there* everything's out front — the screaming and busting things. But rich crazies all sealed shut in their mansion houses are different than that. Slimy, sneaky, everything hidden. That's the McHates. Pretending nothing's the matter, acting like everything's just fine with them. You never know where're you at with rich crazies — they got a special kind of weirdness.

I figure the only time the McHates get along is when they're doing a number on me. Now *that's* gotta be weird.

◆◆◆

Forget about Ivy and the McHates. Talking about them I starts to feel sick. What I really like talking about is my animals, my kennel. Which is why I said okay to living here in the first place. Because of the big yard and the fence and the old shed out back. Not knowing the McHates was laying in wait for me next door. But never mind that.

So, about my kennel. So far I got twelve kittens, four just born. Plus five mothers and two males. That's the cats. Then there's the dogs. I got three of them: a black Lab, one that looks like a small retriever, and Runty, my favourite, a kind of terrier. Looks like Toto from *The Wizard of Oz* only got long ears and a pointy nose.

When welfare first moved us here I went nuts. I says: "How come I gotta live in this shit box when everyone else around here's got it so good?"

Welfare says: "That's all that's available, Sybilla."

"Well, shove it," I says.

Welfare says: "You're lucky you have a place to live, there's people going homeless. But we can always put you up in the Craigmyle Motel till something else comes up."

"The Craigmyle?" I says, "that's a zillion times worse. You want to put me with all those drunks? You want to put little kids with criminals?"

Welfare says: "Well, take your pick, Sybilla. This house is a holding property. Which is why it's available. And the rent is low. You can have the extra money."

So it's the extra money that first done it. But pretty soon it's the big fenced yard, even if the fence is drooping down in places. Because a yard like this means I can have a kennel. Can look after all the stray cats and dogs no one wants.

But the extra money turns out to be a joke. I mean, with all these animals? You got any idea how much it costs to feed them? And the vet bills? Already Dr. Van Horn in town won't see me cause of all the money I owes him. So there's always problems about money. There's never enough. On welfare they gives you about enough to wipe your ass once a day, no more. Here's something, the truth, I swear it: one time a worker told me four rolls of toilet paper oughta be enough for a week so why was I buying more? I don't lie. This was Miss Hope, the public health nurse. I call her Miss Hopeless. A scrunched up broad wearing high heels and bags of make-up. When she found out I bought forty-eight rolls of toilet paper from Shopper's Drug Mart she went nuts. "Sybilla, you have to budget your money," she goes like a teacher. "You have to make it last the whole month. You can't go buying all this toilet paper. What do you need so much toilet paper for, dear?"

"Dear." That's rich. So I goes to her, "Well, dear, there's three of us pooping pretty regular around here and sometimes I have to stuff the baby's diapers with toilet paper because THERE'S NO MORE MONEY FOR PAMPERS and sometimes Christian has an accident, he's only four and a half, and has to be cleaned up." Hoping she'll get the message about the diapers.

But she says, "You should use a wet cloth for Christian. And I've told you before about the diapers, there's no reason the baby can't be wearing cloth ones. It would save you a lot of money if you washed diapers instead of buying them."

Getting nowheres. Like always. Naturally I didn't mention about needing the toilet paper for the cats. There was a bunch of kittens at the time who weren't trained yet and they was messing everywheres. And Miss Hopeless would be going on about the smell if I didn't clean up after *them*. And probably going on about all the animals around here while she was at it, saying like she did one time, how they were causing an UN-WHOLESOME ATMOSPHERE for the kids. So I figures I'd better watch my step, keep my mouth shut. Or she'd be back with a bunch of other workers wanting to take my kids away. And all because I bought too much toilet paper.

◆◆◆

So I'm stuck in the middle of this class-act subdivision, eh? And everyone around here ignoring us, nothing but a bunch of snots, never saying hello to us when we walks by. For a while I figures it's the way I looks with my dyed yellow hair and my high heeled boots. So I wore jeans and runners for a while but it didn't make no difference. People still looked through us like we was invisible. The only ones who has anything to do with us is the McHates. Like lucky us. And Ivy. Poor old Ivy. So we's gots to be content with her.

This one time she invites us over for supper. Says it's her birthday. Says, "Don't even ask me how old I am, I feel like a hundred."

It's a Tuesday night the beginning of December, dark already at four-thirty. The kids and me keep slipping on the mud path out of this dump on the way over. It's so black we can't see nothing but the yellow light in Ivy's kitchen window.

Ivy opens the door looking miserable as usual. She's holding one hand at her back and sighing like she's doing us a big favour inviting us over. So it's weird how she's got her kitchen table all done up if she's feeling this bad. Like for a kid's party. There's a paper table cloth with yellow elephants on it and matching serviettes and paper cups. Plus two white candles in saucers that ain't lit yet.

And I notice she's dressed up, too. Got this flowered dress on with a big pearl broach stuck at her neck and she's curled her thin old hair. She's even wearing red lipstick. And smelling all perfumey like she took a bath in it.

"I didn't tell anyone at Silver Threads it was my birthday," she says. "I didn't want a fuss." I guess that explains why we're invited — no fuss Sybilla.

I gives her my present wrapped in *Snoopy* paper. It's three garden gnomes, two big ones and a little baby one, made of plastic, painted red and blue. I likes them myself, wishing I could have them but they cost too much. Fact is, I've already spent next weeks food money on them.

"You can put them in your garden," I says.

"Some garden," Ivy says, "nothing but weeds, not like it used to be." But she manages to squeeze out one of her creaky smiles saying, "Thank you Sybilla, that was thoughtful."

Next thing we hears a crash from back of the house. And I notice the baby's gone. When we finds her she's screaming, got a cut on her hand from where a lamp fell off Ivy's bedside table and broke. She's okay but Ivy ain't too happy.

"Oh dear, oh dear," she keeps saying, stooping down to pick up the broken bits. "That lamp was a wedding present." Then she starts crying. "I'll go see if I can find a band-aid," she says.

I'm used to Ivy's crying by now so that don't bother me much. It's just that an *aw Christ* kind of feeling comes over me, like everything Sybilla does turns to shit and here's another example. I'm holding the baby and I says to her: "Why can't you leave things alone, you bad girl, see what you've done? You've gone and wrecked Ivy's birthday party." But she starts squirming and hollering so I lets her down.

And have a look around Ivy's bedroom. Except for the broken lamp, everything's neat and clean. There's a big double bed with a shiny purple quilt. Christian starts jumping and sliding off that, having some fun. There's a couple of huge dressers made of dark wood. On one of these there's a birthday card, one of those expensive flowery jobs done in pink and white. It says, *Especially for you, Mother.* Inside it says. "Love Molly & Stan".

When Ivy comes back with the band-aid she catches me looking at the card. "Nice card," I says. "Did Molly send a present?"

"Never you mind," she says, grabbing the card from me.

"What about Arthur? Heard from him?" Arthur's her jerk-off son.

"Arthur's busy with his new job. It's not always easy for him to write."

"What's he gotta write for?" I says, "He lives in the same town."

But Ivy don't want to talk about Arthur. "Supper's ready," she says, putting the quilt back on the bed. "And watch the baby, Sybilla," she says, "we don't want any more accidents."

"Sorry about the lamp," I says.

But Ivy pretends she don't hear me.

So we have this supper and it's not too bad — fried chicken, mashed potatoes, a can of creamed corn. Milk for me and the kids, tea for Ivy. And everything at the table's pretty quiet. Mostly it's the baby falling off her chair with the cushion on it or playing with her food. She's a year and a half won't sit still for no one. Christian, he just eats. Puts his head down and chomps away like he ain't seen food for a week.

When we finish Ivy says she can't get up no more, she's too tired and her legs ache. So I clears the table and gets the cake out of the fridge. It's a Black Forest cake from the bakery. I puts one of the lit candles in the middle of it and me and Christian — well mostly me — sings "Happy Birthday".

I'm handing out the cake when Arthur comes banging at the kitchen door. Like out of nowhere. He's got a card and a pot of brown chrysanthemums that still has the price tag stuck on the plastic cover — $5.95.

"Good timing," he says grinning at me, eyeing the cake.

Ivy looks like she's in shock, like she's just woke up from a long sleep and don't know where she is. Arthur bends over and kisses the side of her face saying *"Happy Birthday."* Then she opens her card, another mushy job, taking a long time reading the verse. "It's lovely," she says. Then struggles out of her chair and goes rooting in the fridge, saying to Arthur, "I know I've got a beer in here somewhere."

Arthur sits down at the table and I hands him a piece of cake. And I'm thinking, what a slimy piece of shit you are. Coming here late with a crappy present, looking all wrecked like you just crawled out of a garbage can. Smelling of booze, half in the bag, and it's only six-thirty. A grown man got to be fifty. A short ass in cowboy boots, wearing long grey hair in a pony tail thinking you're some kind of rock star. I don't look at him or say nothing to him. But starts getting the kids ready to go.

It don't take Ivy two minutes to start complaining, telling him about her pills:

"I'm taking seven different kinds now, Arthur . . . one's for my heart, one's for high blood pressure, one's to help me sleep, one's for pain."

"Uh huh," he says.

Then she looks over at him all sharp and says, "Why haven't you called?"

Arthur's having a smoke, drinking his beer, tilted back on the kitchen chair. He mumbles something about all the work he's doing for Randy and how his phone got cut off because of some hassle with the phone company.

"You should write them a letter," Ivy says all concerned now, "make a formal complaint."

"It wouldn't do no good," he says.

◆◆◆

Stories got a way of telling other stories. So right about here I'm gonna take a little detour. Because people are always asking me about the kids' fathers, eh? And not just workers. Old ladies in the Super Foods, people at bus stops. Like it was their business or something. But okay, I can understand some of that. I can see how people got to be shoving their noses in each other's lives. "Human nature" is what a worker at Alderwood called it: "It's human nature to be interested in other people."

Mostly when I'm asked about the kids' dads I don't say nothing, though, or I make something up. Like how they've got the same dad and he's away working, making bags of money; how he can't wait to get home and buy me a chesterfield, a new TV, a leather jacket. Or I say he's busy building me a house and a kennel, one of those fancy kennels with little heated rooms and music coming outta the ceiling.

So yeah, yeah, I can hear you saying: tell us another one, Sybilla. So all right, here goes: surprise, surprise — the truth is something different. The truth comes out whenever I get in the mood to talk. Like now. Plus I don't want everyone thinking I'm trouble, which I'm not. And the other thing is this: I don't want people siding with the McHates, figuring they're right about Sybilla. I mean the McHates are crazy, slimy perverts like I told you and you'd hate them too if you lived next door. So I'm gonna stop here and tell you some other stuff. It's about guys, and it's this:

Jerk Number One was Christian's dad. He played drums in a rock band called The Magics. His name was Chris which is why I called Christian Christian and not because I'm some out-of-it religious wacko freak. All right? So Christian's named after his dad. So big deal. Like it made any difference? There I was nearly fifteen and hanging around this band and I gets knocked up. But was happy about it. Can you figure that? Stupid or what? Thought I was gonna have a real family or some such shit. Even in the hospital I didn't figure it out. Here comes this guy to visit. A skinny guy with long hair wearing a pink baseball cap turned backwards. And me thinking he was gonna be some kind of daddy. So he gives me a hundred bucks, eh? Right there in the hospital. All twos and fives. "What for?" I says. "For the kid," he says. To get rid of me, I figures out a week later when me and Christian finds him. Got some new girl in his bed. Acting all cold to Christian. Saying: "How do I know it's mine, Sybilla?" Saying: "That baby could be anybody's, anybody's at all."

Jerk Number Two is Jon the Prick, the baby's father. Another skinny guy. Almost looks like a kid himself when he's got his clothes off — thin arms and legs, has this useless moustache made up of about ten hairs. This is the guy Christian figures is his dad, but only because he's been around the longest, nearly six months. The last time we seen Jon was from the back of a cop car. This is the bit that got told about earlier. And I'll tell you why I called the cops that night. Because he was drunk again. Stupid drunk, laughing, acting crazy. And I'd had enough. There it was three in the morning and him telling me he's been out laying carpet (that was his sometime job — carpet layer). So right away I knows there's some girl in the picture and I says: "Don't give me that shit, you've been laying more than carpet." But he won't admit it, says, "Leave me alone, I just wanna sleep." This makes me madder and I starts shaking him, telling him to get out. Okay, okay, I was probably throwing stuff by then, a few plates got broke. But Jon says he ain't going nowheres, tells me to fuck off and tells me this, these are his actual words: "SYBILLA YOU'RE CRAZIER THAN A SHIT HOUSE RAT." So I calls the cops. Tells them there's this asshole bothering me and the kids and he won't leave. So they comes and gets him, eh? And do you think he's given me any money for the baby since? Fat chance. Just a giant transformer toy for Christian's birthday that cost fifty bucks. I know cause I took it back and got the money. I had to tell Christian that Jon the Prick was no good and he won't be seeing him no more. Christian's four and a half. In another couple of years he probably won't even remember him.

So it's a good thing I didn't name the baby after her dad — Jonnie — like I thought of at first. Fact is she's one and a half and don't have a real name yet. Just gets called *The Baby*. Every now and then welfare gets hot about it and says, "Sybilla, you gotta name the baby." Says she can't go through life being called Baby Williams. Why not? I'd like to know. A while back welfare gives me a book of names to look at, then a worker comes by for a visit. An old worker on her last legs, a year short of retirement, Mrs. Blood. Can you beat that for a name? So we have a yak. With Mrs. Blood saying, "What about Heather, that's nice? Or Shannon? Or Jessica? Or Michelle? Or Monica?" And me saying, "Monica? Monica sucks."

So is it my fault if I can't make up my mind? None of the names sounds like her. She's just *The Baby*. And anyways names I come up with always gets shot down. Like Rob, after my invisible dad. Or Oprah, after TV. Or Aviance, the commercial. I even thought of Christine but welfare says that's too much like Christian. "Well," I says, "how 'bout Pepsi?" That was my last suggestion. I said it for a laugh. "Pepsi Williams, after my favourite pop."

Anyways, that's it about the kids and their fathers. That's all I'm gonna say. You know enough already. End of subject. Detour over.

◆◆◆

So it's back to the planet we're on right now. Next thing that happens is welfare calls me up, says, "Sybilla, it's about your animals, we've been getting complaints again." So right away I know who's doing the bitching, eh? The McHates. Every week there's something new. They come stomping over here with the same red faces, standing in front of me spitting and spluttering, saying how so many animals is a health hazard, saying they're FED UP TO THE TEETH with the cat fights, the dog's barking, the whole disgusting sight of the yard. Going on about fleas. Saying how pretty soon the whole neighbourhood's gonna be covered in them. Which is when I start laughing. Like, I wish. This is something I'd give anything to see. All these snot-nosed neighbours covered in fleas, the spiffy women having a million fits about their carpets.

"If we have to call the fumigators because of your fleas," the McHates are screaming at me, "then we're sending you the bill."

"Sure, send me the bill," I tell them, "and watch me put a match to it."

But it looks like the McHates haven't left the complaining just to me. It looks like they've got a petition going. Which is what welfare's calling about now. "There's sixteen signatures," welfare's telling me, "there's too many animals in your front yard."

Too many animals? What are they talking about? I tell welfare to wait on the line, go have a look outside. I count only thirteen cats, most of them sleeping in the dead grass. How can anyone even see them? And the rest of them are in the house. And none of the dogs are outside. They're lying on the living room floor quiet as mice.

"So what's the big deal?" I says to welfare. "It's just the McHatties hassling me again. I'm running a kennel here," I says, "there's supposed to be lots of animals." And slams down the phone. Knowing pretty soon they'll be sending someone over to check things out.

Next day she comes. A new one looks fresh out of welfare school. "Aw right!" I says to Christian, watching her slip through the mud to the front door. A new one probably don't know dick about Sybilla.

She's dressed up like she's going to a wedding, black nylons, expensive beige coat, says her name is Sally. "Come on in, Sally," I says, putting on a big smile. Then I clears the junk off a kitchen chair, tells her to sit down take a load off.

This Sally's shy and nervous, starts making small talk about the kids. Which is what all workers do before they bring out their big guns, get to the point of their visit. Must be the first thing they learn in welfare school — how to butter us up. But I don't give this new one a chance to practice her stuff. Soon as she says the word *animals* I'm off and running, start going on blah blah blah about the dump we gotta live in and how it ain't fit for a rat let alone me and two little kids. And how we should be living in that new housing project over by the airport, Fowler Place, and how I should call up the newspapers and TV, tell them where welfare makes people like me live. TV loves that kind of stuff.

So then she changes the subject, starts asking about the kids' dads which is when I goes into my usual bit about all guys being jerks, good for nothing, only interested in knocking you up then taking off. Then I pull out my big gun which is to ask her personal questions, something every worker hates worse than you and all your problems. Ask her how old she is and does she have any kids yet and is she married or does she have a boyfriend she's shacked up with and where's she living? In some fancy apartment or does she have her own house and how much money does she make, anyway? And how much did her coat cost and her shoes and her car? Which is when she starts grabbing her purse saying she's got another appointment.

I watch her slipping back to the road and get in her car, a Land Rover, and take off like she can't get away fast enough. So long Sally. And I'm feeling pretty good. Having a laugh. Wondering who'll they'll be sending over next.

◆ ◆ ◆

So right after the noise about the petition and the McHates giving me these superior smiles whenever they sees me, I cleans up the yard, figuring to get everyone off my back. I picks up the cat dishes and hacks away at the long grass with an old pair of clippers I finds in the shed. Plus fling handfuls of dog shit into the McHates yard when they ain't looking. I even spend forty bucks on a set of garden gnomes like I got Ivy for her birthday. And puts them around the place.

Things are quiet for a couple of weeks. Meaning the McHates don't come around, meaning welfare's keeping their distance. And then something else starts taking up my time. It's Ivy. Like how she's starting to get strange. And I ain't talking small time crazy like at Alderwood, either, but heavy duty weird. Mental. Because there's no way she'll listen to my problems with the McHates or welfare no more or the stuff about my kennel. Just acts like she's deaf, starts going on about other things.

Then one day she comes over in her dressing gown and slippers in the middle of the afternoon. Walks right in my door without knocking and she's all in a panic. Says she's looking for her husband and children. Says they was here a minute ago and now she can't find them.

I takes her back home saying, "Your husbands are dead Ivy, your kids have buggered off," and she looks at me all confused, and says, "Oh no, we were just having tea and now I can't find them."

Few days later I goes over there and everything's like before. Ivy's all miserable again, this time complaining about her hydro bill saying it's way too high. Saying, "Have you been using my hydro, Sybilla?" Yeah right. Like I'm sneaking over there with an extension cord or something.

Then it's her banging on my door wanting her cookie tray back. "Cookie tray?" I goes. "What cookie tray?"

"You musta taken it," she says, "I can't find it."

❖❖❖

A few weeks after this she phones me up, invites us over for tea. "A tea party," is what she calls it. And me and the kids goes over and she's got the table set with cut out pictures of people sitting on chairs around the table, one picture to a chair. Pictures cut out of magazines. One's an ad for balding hair, two pictures of the same guy, one with hair, one without. Another's a picture of a mom and dad and two kids and a yellow dog standing in front of a Toyota van.

Ivy picks up this picture and kisses it. "My family," she says.

The tea party gets strange. We're drinking out of fancy tea cups I never knew she had and there's cucumber in sandwiches which Christian picks out just eating the bread. Ivy keeps feeding tea to the pictures till they're all wet and you can see through them. Then she wipes them with a napkin, tearing a picture that has big teeth on it, an ad for Crest toothpaste. But Ivy's happy like I never seen her, smiling, talking away to the pictures, ignoring us, saying to the picture of the bald man, "Can I get you another cup of tea?" Saying to the Toyota ad, "Wasn't it wonderful when the snow came and we all went sledding?"

I notice she's got her dining room table set, too, with candles and wine glasses and a long white table cloth. "For my visitors," she says, "I've been so busy with my visitors."

I don't see Ivy for a while after that. There's no sign of her around her house and I starts to feel scared like maybe she's dead in there. Finally I goes over, knocking on the door and listening till I hears some quiet talking. So I goes in. And finds her laying on her bed. She's got a teapot and a couple of cups on her bedside table. And she's got her arms sort of wrapped around this picture beside her. It's a big picture of a man like what you'd see on the back of an expensive book.

"Oh hello Molly," she says, not bothering to get up. "I was just having a nap with lovey. You haven't met my husband Walter, have you?"

After that I calls up welfare.

◆◆◆

Then suddenly there's all kinds of people coming to Ivy's house where before she was a big zero to them, a nothing with a hole in it. There's the public health nurse in one car and a couple of social workers in another. There's a man bringing trays of food, Meals On Wheels, and there's two women from Maids On The Run. A new car drives up with three old women inside and one's carrying some flowers. But they don't stay long.

I goes over after this last crew has left. Ivy's sitting at her kitchen table looking at the card they gave her — *Hope You're Feeling Better*. It's from the Silver Threads. She don't look too bad. Got on her pink sweat suit and is writing out Christmas cards at the kitchen table even though Christmas was three months ago. But she's forgot to eat her lunch. And in the fridge there's a couple more trays, probably yesterday's food. The picture of Walter's sitting on a chair beside her.

It's when she starts wandering off that she gets took away for good. First time one of the people from down the street brings her back. Next time it's the cops. Picking her up on the highway wearing nothing but her slip.

It don't take long for Arthur to move in. Two weeks later he has a garage sale and there's Ivy's stuff set out on tables he's made out of sheets of wood. There's her cups and saucers, vases, a fondue pot, a waffle maker, an old fashioned mixer with three kinds of bowls, sheets and quilts and stuff belonging to her dead husbands — saws, an outboard motor, garden tools, a bunch of tin.

Arthur's having a great time wandering around hauling in the money. There's cars parked up and down the street and people hurrying to the tables afraid they'll miss out on something good. Everyone's picking over stuff, asking Arthur, "How much, how much?" The McHates go off with a shovel and a couple of pails, maybe to clean up the dog shit I recently gave them.

I gets some plastic bowls for feeding the animals and an ornament of a girl holding an umbrella. For some reason it reminds me of Ivy. I put a sign on my fence too, KITTENS FOR SALE, $5 EACH and sell all but two making thirty-five bucks.

The garage sale goes on all weekend. By now Arthur's driving Ivy's car, must of figured he's died and gone to heaven. His old pickup's parked in the driveway. And he don't bother putting Ivy's car in the garage either. Pretty soon it's covered in grunge just the way he likes it.

And the house? You'd figure he'd be having parties, raising shit. But he ain't. It's quiet over there, like before, hardly anyone visiting. At night I can see the light coming from the TV. And he never comes out of the house before noon. Must be up all night with the box, sleeping most of the day away.

◆ ◆ ◆

What happens next like blows me away. Welfare calls me up and says, "Sybilla, how'd you like to move to Fowler Place?" Just like that. Like thud. It takes a minute to sink in. "A vacancy in Fowler Place?" I says.

"That's right," they says. "You can move the end of the month. But we need to know if you're interested."

"Interested?" I says. "I can be ready in five minutes. Just pile everything in the yard set a match to it."

"Only thing," welfare says, "you can't take all your animals with you. Only one cat and one dog no more than thirty pounds. You'll have to find homes for the others."

So right away there's the catch, the good mixed with the bad, the way all workers operate. But I knows the game. You know what I'm saying? So I says about the animals: "Yeah, sure, whatever you say." And gets onto other things. Like how I'll be needing new furniture for Fowler Place, the stuff I've got's so wrecked. "And while you're at it," I says, "what about a new TV, mine's got wavy lines. You can't expect us to watch TV with wavy lines, can you?" And welfare says they'll see what they can do.

◆◆◆

Week before we move, me and the kids visit Ivy at the personal care home. Let me say one thing right now: shoot yourself before you get put in a place like this. A one story building crammed with old people wandering the halls or sitting tied in chairs not knowing which end is up. And everything smelling of bleach and boiled vegetables.

First we go looking for Ivy in her room. They tell us at the desk it's way down the hall. Every door we pass has a big piece of paper pinned beside it with a picture of who lives inside and some words about who they are. Like this: *Mrs. Nelson studied nursing but never practiced. No children.* And *Mrs. Sampson has three children and seven grandchildren. She likes to help others.* And *Mr. Creedle worked on the boats. He enjoys watching TV and likes a good joke.* Outside Ivy's door it says: *Mrs. Harrison has two children and three grandchildren. She enjoys playing Bingo.* Ivy's picture don't look like her, she's got curly hair, they must of permed it.

Inside Ivy's room there's a bed, a TV, a brown easy chair, and a bunch of pictures in frames — school pictures of kids, the grandchildren, I guess, and a strange picture of Arthur taken when he graduated from high school a million years ago, looking young and ugly. There's a picture of Molly in a ski outfit. But no Ivy.

We find her in the activity room where there's a piano, a bunch of tables, and windows so high up you think you're in a basement. On the bulletin board there's a poster that says COME TO THE EASTER CAROL SING-A-LONG ON THE 15TH. There's cut out flowers pasted on the walls. It looks like a kid's classroom in there.

Ivy's sitting at a table with a bunch of other old women looking at magazines but she don't know me. "Who?" she keeps saying, "who?" And the activity worker's whispering to me: "She doesn't recognize anyone since she had the stroke."

❖❖❖

So here we are, it's moving day. Me and Christian and the baby, we're sitting at the kitchen table waiting for welfare to pick us up. We got four garbage bags filled with clothes and a bunch of boxes filled with Christian's toys and dishes and blankets. And we got the plastic garden gnomes; I figure they'll look good on the front porch at Fowler Place. Welfare's sending round a truck for the baby's crib and the beds and this table we're sitting at. At Fowler Place there's a new chesterfield waiting for us. And a new TV. Runty's here, and Gimp, my favourite cat. They get to go with us. Gimp's pregnant but welfare don't need to know about that. The last two kittens I sold out front the liquor store last weekend. And some lady with four kids took both the other dogs. They was sitting out front the liquor store with us. When I told her kids they was gonna be put to sleep if I couldn't find them a home, they went to work on their mom. So she took them. The other cats went to the S.P.C.A. I don't even want to think what'll happen to them there. I promised Christian one of Gimp's kittens when they're borned so he'd quit crying about the other cats. I promised he could pick any one he wanted.

The McHates haven't showed their face. I hope they kill each other.

And me? I'm outta here. Just like that.

KEEP THIS AND NEVER LOSE IT

*F*irst time I seen Fowler Place was on a poster at the welfare office. A giant poster taking up most of one wall in the waiting room. On it was a drawing of a bunch of white buildings with grass around them and blue sky and a few white clouds up above. A couple of cars parked in the driveway and stick people walking in one of the doors. Fowler Place looked beautiful, like a hotel. And I wanted to live there.

The day Welfare moves us in is the first time I seen it live. And guess what? It don't look nothing like the poster. Not nearly so big and not all white but brown with green and white trim like any other cheap apartment building. Plus it was raining that day so there was no blue sky either. But the main thing about it was the airport. Fowler Place is on this flat land beside the airport and there ain't any other houses around. You take the airport road. Then about a mile before you get to the airport gate there's this cut-off to Fowler Place. And that's it: six four-plexes with a fence around it plunked down in the middle of an empty field. It looked like a prison. I says to Welfare before we even gets out of the car: "How're we supposed to get to town living way out here? I mean what about busses? You think I got a car hid in my bag or something?"

So all the excitement about moving goes flat and I'm feeling pissed off, almost to bawling. Even when we gets inside I don't hardly cheer up. Our place is Number 22 in the four-plex farthest from the road and parking lot. Well, okay, I'll say it if you twist my arm: it's pretty nice inside. Compared to the dump we come from. And if you likes the colour beige which is everywhere — on the floors, the walls, even on the new chesterfield which Welfare promised us when we moved in. The only different colour in the place is on the kitchen cupboards: white with peach trim.

But there's a new TV in the living room. I'll say this much for Welfare: they made good on their promise about getting us a new TV. Right away I turns it on make sure it's working — Oprah talking to three child molesters. Then Christian goes running up the stairs and me and the baby follows him. There's two bedrooms up there and more of that beige. Christian's bed and the baby's crib has been set up in one room, and my old wrecked double's in the other. Upstairs is where the bathroom is, too, with a tub and shower. I turns on all the taps make sure they run.

Back downstairs I looks in the fridge. And sees it's got food inside — milk, margarine, a few apples, a loaf of bread, and some Kraft singles. That's it. So I says to Welfare carrying in our stuff from the car, this old guy worker got a droopy grey moustache, "What're we supposed to eat?" And he says, "Didn't they talk to you about getting groceries?" And I goes, "Like what are you talking about? No-one's talked to us about dick. Just that this is moving day and be ready at 1." So then this Welfare guy looks at his watch, gives a big sigh, and grabs the phone in the kitchen which ain't hooked up yet. "Oh," he says, surprised, the bell going off in his head when he figures out it's dead. Then he says, "I'll get the office to order you pizza for tonight. Someone will be around tomorrow."

Next day Welfare takes us to Safeway, tells me the airport bus stops at the Fowler Place entrance. And gives me a schedule.

◆◆◆

So here we are at Fowler Place might as well be on the moon. Soon as the phone gets working I calls up my best friend Cindy at her aunt's house want to tell her my news. Tell her maybe she can bring her kid George and move here too. Live next door or something cause it's real lonely out here. So far only a few of the places has people in them, a couple of old ladies, a couple of families with older kids never around. I could sure use Cindy's company.

But her aunt's phone on the reserve ain't working, it's disconnected again. Which is no surprise. Most of the time it ain't working. And fact is I don't even know if Cindy's at her aunt's place no more. She could of taken off again, followed that idiot boyfriend of hers up the coast to his reserve. What a lost cause that is. Like Jason Jimmy's got two screws missing. He's a nut case and I don't mean peanuts. His elevator don't go to the top. But Cindy says that's my opinion and gets pissed off when I talk about him like that. Says he ain't so bad, he only gets drunk, don't beat her up or nothing. Just does stupid stuff like tries to lasso cop cars, or jumps off cliffs into the ocean in the middle of the night when he's all juiced up. Or gets into fights with white guys at the Rec Centre when it's Friday night skate.

"Well, okay," I says, "maybe he don't beat you up or nothing but what does he do that's good? Like does he give you money for George his real and only kid that we know of? And is he ever nice to you, do things for you like buy you presents for your birthday, or look after you when you're sick? Answer me that," I says. "Always screwing around with some other girl, white or indian don't make no difference, and bringing them back to where you're staying, acting proud like he's a cat just bagged a rat? What's so great about that? And what about the time he tried to get you to screw his baseball team," I says, "the whole team and they was drunk and banging on the side of your aunt's house, all fifteen of them, and your aunt had to call the cops and there was that big fight and everyone landed in jail for the night even you and your aunt cause you ended up taking their side against the cops? What about that?"

But Cindy always says when I get to this part, "Fuck off Sybilla," in this low hard voice, and gets scrunched up in her face so I don't push it no more. Cindy's two hundred pounds five foot one and can be mean when she wants to. I seen it loads of times at Alderwood. The way she'd punch the workers. Or flatten other kids with just one arm. Wham. They'd be out of action for a week. Too bad she don't do that to Jason Jimmy. The skinny runt. She could wipe him out easy.

So it's "Fuck off Sybilla" when I starts going on about Jason Jimmy. And it's Cindy getting twisted saying, "You don't take no prize, Sybilla." Meaning with guys. Meaning if there was a contest for sticking with guys I'd come in last.

Like in the beauty contests on TV. Where they have prizes for girls that don't get to be queen or princess. Like Miss Personality. And Miss Takes a Good Picture. And Miss Helpful to Others. That's the one that slays me. Why would you want to help other girls win the contest? I've never figured that one out. In the Miss World contest when they announce the finalists all the other girls run over squealing to hug and kiss them. Why would they wanna do that? It's so fake. Anyone can see they're about ready to bawl their eyes out and given half a chance maybe tear at the winner's dress or pull out her hair. I would in a flash. If that was me on stage I'd be running from the back row and grabbing the queen's crown. I'd be screaming at the judges: "You shoulda picked me, this queen sucks, she's screwed just about every guy in sight to get this crown." That's what I'd be yelling.

It's the truth. That's what these contests are about: seeing how far you can get by jerking off the right guys. Me, I'm always picking the wrong guys so end up nowheres; there's no crown for me. Ever. Story of my life. Cindy's right, I ain't winning no contest. But I got a real talent — I was born with it. Like some people are good at playing the guitar or being hairdressers. Me, I got talent when it comes to guys. Zeroing in on the assholes. Always falling for a good looking face or a smooth line. When all along there's another major idiot just waiting to screw me over. What's the matter with me anyhow? How come it keeps happening? Because I'm always hoping the next guy will be okay. So wake up and smell the smoke, Sybilla, when has that ever happened? Miss Walking Disaster. That's me. That's the prize I'd get if there was a contest. Cindy'd be Miss Hole In The Head on account of Jason Jimmy. But me, I'd be Miss Walking Disaster — Collector of Assholes.

I could open up a store there's been so many. And call it the Museum of Assholes. Have all these guys stuffed like fish hanging on the walls. Give guided tours.

When I told Cindy this she didn't laugh. "What's so funny about that?" she said, "you can't make the whole world into a store."

She's right, you wouldn't find a store big enough. She also said, "Smarten up, Sybilla, you wanna get AIDS and die?"

Cindy says my problem is I'm addicted to guys. She says there oughta be some kind of clinic for people like me, like where addicts go to come off booze or dope. Some kind of sex clinic where they teach you to quit thinking about guys. A place filled with nothing but nerds wearing their pants up to their armpits, and short sleeved white shirts. That'd cure me, she says. But it's more than that, the screwing around, I tell her. It's the good times I has with guys at the beginning, the laughs and everything, the going places, eating out and taking the kids along. And me pretending we're a family. The way I likes to watch other people watching us, maybe thinking to themselves: "There's a nice family, what a pretty young mother she is and ain't the kids cute." This gives me a real charge. Not the way everyone usually stares at us when we're alone. Like we're a parade of slime balls.

Mark, this worker at Alderwood used to get on my case because I did this all the time. Pretend things. Daydreaming, he called it. "Get in the real world, Sybilla," he'd say. He'd say: "Earth to Sybilla, anybody home?" Knocking on my head like it was a door.

What this Mark didn't know was the dreams were about him. At least I don't think he knew. He was some good looking guy, had wavy blond hair and not old like some of the workers, maybe twenty-two or twenty-three when I was twelve.

I didn't have tits or nothing back then. A real twerp, looked about nine or ten, skinny as a broom. But I kept thinking all this goopy stuff about Mark. That we loved each other but had to keep it secret because of him being a worker and me being a kid. So I'd write him letters and hide them in his coat pocket. Disguise the way I wrote and didn't sign my name. And when it was his turn to sleep over I'd make myself throw up so's he'd have to look after me. Have to lie on my bed and read me something out of a book. One time I made a picture of him and me holding hands in this garden. We were flowers and our hands were leaves and there was these two black spiders either side of us standing guard. On top of the picture I writes "KEEP THIS AND NEVER LOSE IT."

Naturally what happens next is he gets transferred. The supervisor makes up some story blah dee blah about Mark getting a shift leader job in the next house. Thinking I'm stupid, don't know what's going on, trying to keep us apart. I raised a stink about his moving, threw some chairs around and a pot through the dining room window. Didn't do no good. "An inappropriate relationship" was the words they used: What a load! So after Mark moves he gets cool to me, nice but cool, like the receptionist at the welfare office. The supervisor must of been in control of his brain or something. Suddenly he's too busy for me, he's got other kids to think about. Then I sees him walking down the driveway holding hands with a trainee worker called Kim.

So am I breaking your heart yet? Time to bring out the violins?

Don't laugh. I'm serious. Like that song — "Looking for Love In All the Wrong Places". What I want to know is: where's the right places?

Trouble is I sees guys all over the place. And most of them looks good to me. Yeah, yeah, I tries to be careful. Tries to CONTROL myself. THINK TWICE. On account of diseases. Like workers have said to me a zillion times: "Think twice before you act Sybilla and you won't get in so much trouble."

Which is what I'm trying to do now. Because of this guy I keeps seeing on my trips to town. Trying to think twice before I makes a move. He's a dude kind of guy. Big hair, big shoes, tight jeans. I sees him waiting out front the bank or walking along by Safeway going into the liquor store. And once I seen him in Shopper's looking at the wall of shampoos. I hung around looking at the deodorants further down trying to watch him, see what kind of shampoo he takes, but the baby runs off and I has to catch her. Time I get back he's gone.

I likes this guy. How come? Because of they way he looks. And what I get in my head about the way he is. He's skinny, not too tall, don't have a beard or moustache. I hate beards. Cause of all the junk that gets stuck in them.

Anywho, I figure this guy's into music. I can tell because of Christian's dad; he played in a band. In a way this new guy reminds me of him. The way he walks. The way his hands hang down like he's resting them from all that guitar playing. I likes guitar playing the best. All the videos on *Much Music* show these guys with bare arms and long hair, wearing their leather pants up on stage. And everyone in the crowd screaming, waving their arms. So cool.

But about this new guy . . . so far I'm just looking. I don't know if he's noticed me or not; so far I haven't got his eye. Cindy's always saying to me, "Sybilla, who's gonna want you with two little kids?" Then she goes, "Sybilla, you better watch it, next thing you'll be knocked up again and for sure no one will want you then."

"What makes you so smart?" I says to her, "what makes you the big expert?" And we gets into another hassle about the useless Jason Jimmy. So I'm getting nowheres with guys. And the ones I even have a conversation with are doorknobs.

But I wish Cindy was around. My best friend in the world. I wish she was sitting at my kitchen table right now. With George crawling around on the floor playing with the baby and us laughing it up drinking Pepsi or maybe beer if we has the money. Because I'd be telling her what happened a while back.

How me and the kids are walking through the mall when this guy calls me over, says, "Hey Sybilla."

I looks over to where he's sitting. In the cafeteria section where there's about fifteen different take-out stands spread around a bunch of plastic tables and stools in the middle. This guy's sitting at one of the tables in the smoking section, drinking out of a paper cup that says *Muffin Break*. He's dirty looking, fat, has a greasy beard, greasy clothes. He waves me over. I don't recognize him at first. Then I do.

"It's me Davey," he says. "Remember me? From Alderwood?"

"Sure I remember," I says, not exactly thrilled at seeing him. A real wimp is what I'm remembering, always screaming over nothing, then bawling when one of the workers yells at him. A bag of wind. Was into knives back then, and guns. The workers put him in the cadets but he got kicked out for stealing ammunition. Be about twenty-one, twenty-two by now.

I sits down at the table, puts the baby on my lap, says to him, "So how ya doin Davey?"

"Great," he says, and don't waste no time telling. Says, "I've had the same job for three years now. Over at the Tire Shop. I'm on my coffee break. I come here every day. Shit, you don't look any different. Skinny as ever." And he's grinning, says, "Remember the time you and Alan Kamouroski started that fire on Halloween? That was so cool."

"Yeah," I says, "yeah."

Then he tells me more stuff. That he's got his own apartment, living by himself over on Quadra street. That he's got a big Sony TV with a twenty-eight inch screen. That there's no one special in his life, he's not ready for the big commitment, not yet. That he's still got his motorcycle, not the Harley anymore since his wreck but something okay for riding around town. All the time picking his paper cup to bits.

Yawn. Yawn. Yawn.

"Hard to figure where the time's gone," he says. "Hey, I saw Kathy a couple of years back. She was living down the road from me, on welfare, had about four kids. And did you hear about Alan Kamouroski being in jail? Stupid bugger. Burned down his doctor's office. And Barbara? I heard she's hooking in Vancouver."

"I heard she's dead."

"No shit."

"Yeah, Cindy told me. OD'ed on something."

"Oh fuck, Cindy. I'd forgotten about her. Still a lard ass?"

"She's on a diet."

"Remember the time she broke my arm? Jesus, she was tough." And he's grinning some more. Offers me a cigarette, Players Filter.

"Thanks," I says, taking it. "I gotta go."

"No wait," he says, all worried, reaching across the table, grabbing my arm. "What's the rush? Sit down, take a load off."

So I sits back down. Then Davey says, "Hear what happened to Murray?"

Murray was a worker at Alderwood, used to play with us, tag and Gila Monster out on the playfort, and hide and seek in the woods. For hours and hours. An old guy, had a beard, grey hair. One time I heard him in the staffroom going nuts at the supervisor. Heard him screaming this at the top of his lungs: "Don't fuck with my feelings." Then watched him come crashing out of the room, and go running through the house, his face all red, knocking over a lamp on his way outside.

"No," I says, "what happened to Murray?"

"He went crazy," Davey says, and he's looking freaked. "That really bothered me when I found out. I mean he was just like a father to me and then he went nuts. Had to be put in the bug house. He was the best worker I ever had. I'm still trying to figure out why he went crazy. It really bothers me."

"Huh," I says. Then there's silence. "I really gotta go," I says, "the baby's hungry." Though for once she's being quiet on my lap and Christian's happy twirling on one of the stools.

"You got a guy?" Davey says.

"Yeah," I says, "we're gonna get married this Christmas. He's building me a house. He's in the construction business. Got loads of money."

"No shit."

"Yeah, and we're gonna start a kennel for cats and dogs. We've got a bunch of animals already."

"You guys oughta come round for a visit sometime. Bring a girlfriend. You know, like for me."

"Yeah, sure."

"Know what?" he says as I'm leaving. "I figure I'm one of the ones that made it. All those others? Kathy, Alan, Barbara? They never made it to first base. Me, I did. After six foster homes, three group homes and Alderwood, I made it okay. All those workers? They musta been doing something right. I mean, I got morals now. I figure that's what I was missing all those years ago. Morals."

I don't say nothing.

"You made it too," he says. "I can tell just by looking at you."

Part II

Word of Mouth

"We must invent the heart of things if we wish one day to discover it."

— Sartre

Refusal

SLAP

*F*irst there was a slap. Two slaps, one on either cheek. *Don't interrupt me when I'm on the phone!* Slaps you'd see a princess give a nobody in a movie, or a maid, or a workman. Smack, smack. Like that. Quick. With the hand that fed, that washed the body, that brushed the hair. Slaps like the sound of sudden gunfire, unpredictable. And the war zone: the living room, the narrow hallway where the telephone rang.

She must have placed the phone under her chin, must have positioned it carefully so she could slap with ease. *Come here while I slap you.* No, it was the pulling at her skirt, at the long slim high-heeled legs that did it. Close enough for her to whirl around, one hand free. And a dummy child in place to receive it, not figuring it out in time, always too close, always surprised and shocked. A sudden slap like the slap of birth, or of insight.

ANGELS

*T*here's a house at the foot of a steep hill, a rented house with dusty passageways and hidden rooms, with balconies overlooking a large wood-panelled living room, a castle of a house. In an upstairs bedroom there are angels. Yes, angels, you're sure of it. Three in white gowns, two in blue, with thick, waxy wings. Hovering at the end of your bed; one is floating near the ceiling, its golden hair brushing the overhead light. Angels living — if that's what angels do — in your room. They don't speak but their presence is so claustrophobic you scream. Scream and scream. Their presence is sucking the air from the room, but they're smiling at you warmly, like Bible drawings of Jesus, and their smiles never change. Smiling while they eat your air.

Quit imagining things, you're later told. *Come down to earth.*

CAKE

You've never had a birthday party before. A few neighbourhood children are invited. They're pastel shadows, a knot of frenzy playing musical chairs in a living room as big as Cinderella's Ball Room. The music's "The Teddy Bears' Picnic": *When you go down to the woods today you're in for a big surprise!*

There's balloons and a Birthday cake, white with pink icing. *Happy Birthday to you.* It comes in a box from a store. *Don't expect me to make a cake, I wouldn't know how.* The cake is sliced and handed round. *One for you, one for you.* A rush of children crowd round the long table. They're agitated, grabbing. You stand apart, refusing your slice. No one seems to notice.

Even that night, long past the party when you're sitting on a babysitter's lap in the kitchen, the last of the cake on the table before you, you still refuse. You're breaking your heart for a piece of that cake but you won't touch it. *Go on, just a lick, it won't bite you.* Instead you take hold of a kitchen knife and chop the cake into crumbly pieces, making a collapsed castle surrounded by mounds of icing that look like melted mountains. You imagine the babysitter allowing this careful destruction, allowing the cake to wait on the table for midnight. Midnight when the woman returns with the Father. There's a Father? Yes, somewhere then.

The woman comes into the kitchen with the Father and sees the ruined cake. You imagine she cares.

BEDROOM

Each night it must be dark outside before you'll go to bed; only then will the angels float into the bedroom shadows — into the closet, beneath the bed, on the dark side of the dresser. Only at night do you have enough room to bounce on the bed, to dance, to swing your arms and spin in circles without touching the angels. But even so, you feel their weight. Like a pressure on your chest. Like a huge ball hurling through space, a ball too wide for your grasp, a ball you're barely able to hold on to. Because there's always the danger of sliding off.

During the daytime you must make yourself small enough to squeeze past the angel's thick wings which smell of grease, around their heavy gowns that settle over the bedroom furniture like lava.

Afraid of touching them because what would happen then?

HANDLESS

*T*his woman who slaps. What of her? Oh, you keep away from her, at least you try, keep her at arm's length, refused. Because a nightmare is having your arms cut off below the elbows. There's so much blood when you push her away. But still she grabs, still she slaps.

Why won't you call her Mother? Because the word sticks hard in your throat like a growl and won't form into music.

Instead, you call her the slapping woman.

BROWN

What does the slapping woman look like? Is she beautiful? Is she a beautiful, wicked Queen? No, not beautiful though she has a certain grace, like the cold stiffness of a China figurine.

But everything about her is brown. Like dirt? Yes, like dirt. From her thin hair to her dull-brown eyes, from her tailored suits and her alligator high-heeled shoes to the twin fox-furs she wears when going out, draped around her shoulders like a live thing. Two tiny fox heads with yellow glass eyes staring at you from either side of her neck.

MUD PIES

*I*n the backyard you mould the slapping woman out of mud and twigs, a whole family of mud-pie women, some larger and more fierce than the others, some small and helpless. When the mud is powdery dry, you have wars with them, smashing them together until they crumble, until armies of perishing slapping women are strewn in broken clumps about the ground.

You use twigs for their arms and legs because her bones are so sharp they hurt you when you're held. Twigs that snap easily in half, then snap in half again.

LAPS

*T*ea in the living room. She pulls you onto her lap in front of a neighbour woman. Her knees are sharp through her brown skirt; it's difficult to balance, to sit still without falling off.

She's being careful with you, formal, slow. No, you couldn't call it kindness, but her voice is even, a silky veil, a kind of song. She's talking to the woman about her home, far away, across the ocean. *The sun shines all the time in Australia. Just shines and shines. Not like here where there's nothing but rain.*

Warily you let her hold you, soothed by the delicious sound of her newly soft voice.

Her slapping hands for the moment lying still.

MUSIC

A crowd of strangers with drinks in their hands have gathered around the piano at the far end of the living room. The slapping woman is playing "Kitten on the Keys", "The Twelfth Street Rag", "Hernando's Hide-Away". Everyone is singing. You're sitting on the piano bench beside her plunking at the high end of the keyboard, at those shrill notes that are never used. Miraculously you're at the heart of things, ignored.

Once during these times she calls you *Darling* and strokes your hair. Darling!

Play us another one Nancy. Something we can get our teeth into. Play "Too-Ra-Loo-Ra-Loo-Ra". Play "My Heart Is Like A Red Red Rose."

Darling! The music of that rare caress.

THE FATHER

She's given him your plate with the cut-up meat. Then laughs and laughs. Standing at his side, she's feeding him the meat, one piece at a time. *Be a good boy and eat your supper!* And he's laughing too, his head's thrown back, his wide mouth open. Oh, the bells of that private laughter! His paper napkin at his throat like a bib. He's holding his mouth like a hungry bird, she's teasing him with the meat. *Don't be a naughty boy!* Making him bend after it, further and further, until he falls off the chair.

PRISON

*T*he slapping woman is shouting. Throwing plates of food against the kitchen cupboards, a bowl of stewed prunes, a gravy boat against the kitchen door after the father's retreating back. A white door, brown gravy.

Once again she's crying. *I want to go home. I hate this country, and all this rain. It's a prison. I hate everything about it.*

SAILORS

*D*ressed in a nightgown, you're running circles around the edge of the living room rug, jumping on the armchairs, keeping time to "The Teddy Bears' Picnic". Play the record again! And again! The Father's on the floor beneath a lamp holding a needle and pink thread, sewing doll's underpants. And a cape! And a doll's skirt made from a piece of cut-up pillowcase. Threading elastic with a safety pin through a crude wasteband. *I learned how to sew at sea, on the ships at night. We had to do our own mending.*

You're sitting on the living room rug with the Father eating toast and jam. Then the floor's a heaving black ocean with orange circle islands made from the light of table lamps and you're a sailor hopping from one circle to the next. *Yo ho ho.* The Father's clapping his hands. *And a bottle of rum.*

GONE

Where is the slapping woman?
She's gone.
Gone like a drifting fog because her departure is so quiet. She's slipped out at night, floated through the bedroom ceiling with the angels.

You've looked up from your playing, turned around at the supper table and she's not there. You weren't watching and she stole away. You weren't watching and she's slapped you again.

BOAT

Why won't you eat? The Father's given you all your favourite foods: chocolate cake and ice cream, fish and chips, orange pop, jelly beans, marshmallows. You should be happy; this should be a celebration, she's gone away. Why won't you speak? *Cat got your tongue?*

But there are no words for this emptiness, it's too large to name. You long for her slippery legs, for the hands that once stroked your hair. Without her presence you feel eerily alone.

The Father rocks you on his lap. He reads to you: *Winnie the Pooh, The Owl and The Pussycat.* You cry and cry, adrift in your sadness. You're clinging to a ball that's too wide for your grasp. Hold onto the Father, he's a sailor, he won't let you drown. Listen he's telling you a story: *She's gone away on a boat, maybe never to return.*

She's sailed in a boat, in a pea-green boat, she's slapping the ocean blue.

FACE

*H*overing, he's nervous like a bird. Always near. Playing Pick Up Sticks with you, cutting out paper dolls. Pushing you on a swing at the park, pushing you so high you can see over the tops of trees, can glimpse the far off bay and the tiny boats bound for China.

Strange how you'd never noticed how large his nose is, how bright his blue eyes. Or his hair. The way dark strands are combed over his bald head.

You sleep on the living room chesterfield now, refusing to enter your room upstairs, afraid of what the angels might do now that the slapping woman has gone. Will they be mad at you? Punish you finally, crush you beneath their heavy wings?

At bedtime the Father kisses you on the forehead. *Sleep tight. Don't let the bed bugs bite.*

BOOK

*I*n the living room of the castle house. You're helping the Father put toys into a large cardboard box.

And where will I love?

You mean live?

Yes, where will I live?

With your Aunt Alice on the Island. And I'll visit every weekend. You can make me toast and jam, and we'll take rides in the car and go to the beach.

And stand on the shore, and wave at the waves, and stare at the boats in the distance.

And what about your tricycle? Do you want to take that?

Oh yes. And the doll and the doll's clothes and all the books. Hans Christian Andersen. *The Princess and the Pea. The Snow Queen.* The Snow Queen! *There once was a child who lived frozen inside . . .*

Pushing aside the toys you take hold of the Father's hand.

Secrets

WRONG

About Nancy and Billy — what happened between them was too bad though we knew it wouldn't last. Because my brother, your dad, was a homebody. What he wanted was a family, a quiet life. What your mother wanted was to be the belle of the ball, go out dancing and drinking. She loved spending money and having a good time. She'd leave you with anybody if there was a party to go to. Your dad would rather read a book. So they were wrong for each other. This was plain to everyone but Billy. Nancy left him three times in the space of five years and went back to Australia each time. After the last time you came to live with Arnie and me, with our family. Billy went back to being a bachelor. And he closed up. You couldn't get him to say two words about Nancy. All his attention went to you; he worked on the boats in Vancouver and every other weekend for thirteen years he came over to the Island. He never missed a weekend. He said to me one time, early on, "Having kids gives you something to live for." It gave me the creeps when he said this. So I was happy if he clammed up about his life. I couldn't stand morbid talk.

But it's stories you're wanting.

FIRST MEETING

Out of nowhere we got a letter from Billy in Australia saying he'd just got married. This caused a lot of excitement because the family always figured Billy would stay a bachelor; he was the quiet type, a hard worker. The letter also said he'd rented a house in Sydney for his new wife, that there was a baby on the way.

This happened just after we'd moved into the house on Leslie Drive, the house Arnie built. We'd lived in the basement for several months while Arnie finished the upstairs but I didn't complain. The house was at the top of a hill. It had wood shingles painted green and two big picture windows either side of the front door so it looked like a house a kid might draw at school. And every tree had been cleared off the lot. I was proud of that because this made the house modern; trees and bushes were for houses in the sticks. Later on we put a fish pond in the back yard.

The first time I saw Nancy she was wearing a long blue coat with a silver fox fur draped around her neck and a blue felt hat with net that came down over her eyes. Very swish looking, very sophisticated. I thought: this can't be my brother's wife; she's too grand a lady for him. Because he was so quiet. But there was nothing quiet about her. Loud, she was, and forward. Took one look around our place, plunked herself down on a chair and said, "Well, where's the cocktails?"

It was like some fancy bird had landed in my kitchen; nobody knew what to do. Cocktails! In the middle of the day! She made everybody shy.

You were about six months old at the time, a pretty baby, but I noticed that day it was Billy, your dad, who was holding you, doing all the fussing. Nancy had nothing to do with you apart from sticking a bottle in your mouth. Billy even changed you. She couldn't have cared less if you were screaming or dirty. That first day she was more interested in getting Arnie to fix her cigarette lighter which had broke, and showing off her fox fur to my girls. She never did get her cocktail, either; we didn't have that sort of thing in the house. She had to be content with a cup of weak tea.

The three of you stayed at Grandma's but before the week was up, Nancy had gone off with Billy on one of his cruises. Officer's wives could do that then, accompany their husbands on the boats. You got left behind with me. They were gone two weeks.

We liked having a baby in the house; Arnie and me were too old to have another of our own. And the girls — they'd be about eleven and fourteen at the time — they liked dressing you up, taking you for walks. When Nancy came and got you everyone was sad.

HEART

When you were three I got you for a year. Nancy said she needed to visit her family in Australia. A two month trip, she said, leaving your dad in Vancouver working on the boats, leaving you with me. For two months we didn't hear nothing from her and then we got a telegram saying her mother was sick and she had to stay longer. Six months went by and she sent two more telegrams, making excuses why she couldn't return. I'd say to Billy, "When's Nancy coming back?" And he'd shrug his shoulders. "In the fall," he'd say, or "In the spring," depending on how many months had gone by. Then he wouldn't talk about it.

Finally, after a year, she turned up. We didn't know she was coming. Maybe your dad knew but he didn't say nothing to me. She showed up in a taxi, dressed to the nines. Coming into the house and kissing everyone hello like it had been only two weeks since we'd seen her. When she tried to pick you up you screamed and hung onto my leg; she had to pry you away. You didn't know who she was. But right away she took you to Vancouver, to a house Billy had rented in Kerisdale. I cried for two days and two nights.

When you were gone a week Nancy phoned me. "I can't do nothing with Judy," she said. "She won't eat, she won't play, she just sits on the chesterfield staring out the window."

I wanted to go over but Arnie wouldn't let me. "You'll only go through it again," he said.

It broke my heart. She took everything when she took you. The high chair, your three-wheeled bike. I had to wrap your mug and spoon in paper for the boat ride to Vancouver and I cried the whole time. But there was nothing I could do. You belonged to her.

Then a month later you had your fourth birthday and Arnie and I went over to visit. You didn't even have a dress to wear. There you were, running around the house all day in your nightie. I went out and bought you some clothes.

After that Nancy took you back to Australia, left your dad and we didn't hear nothing from her for a year and a half.

A WOMAN CALLED BO

Then suddenly Nancy turns up and calls from Vancouver. "I'm back," she says, just like she'd been out shopping, "We're coming over to visit."

The next day she arrives with you and a woman called Bo, someone she met in Australia. Bo wore men's pants and a brown leather belt with a Girl Guide belt buckle. She had short, straight hair, wore sweater sets but had nothing to show up top. Men's shoe's, too, black Oxfords. It seems this Bo was travelling with your mother. She'd been in the army in Australia.

Nancy was another thing. Dressed to kill. My girls were taken with her plastic high-heeled shoes, the latest thing. They had dice floating in some liquid in the heel — see through heels. And a full length mink coat with a mink hat to match that must have cost your dad a penny. And angora sweaters, the girls loved those. So Nancy made a big impression. In those days I was still making over old coats for the girls; there wasn't a lot of money to go around. The girls thought Nancy was a movie star.

You and Nancy went to my sister Gracie's house; we put a cot in my girls room for Bo.

For a few days things didn't go too bad, visiting and that. Gracie was left to do most of the cooking as if she didn't have enough on her hands what with being a widow and having Grandma and her layabout son Larry living with her. Twenty-three or four Larry was and not working, always fiddling with his motorcycle. Don't ever ask him to take out the garbage! So

Gracie had her hands full. But I made brownies and cookies and took them over, and another time a pot of stew which Bo turned her nose up at. Seems she'd only eat lamb or chicken, no beef.

It was a morning after the girls had gone to school and Arnie had gone to work. And Bo comes into the kitchen. I was at the counter making pastry. My hands were covered in flour and Bo comes up behind me and puts her arms around me. "I like you, Alice," she says. I was shocked. I washed my hands and went outside and sat on the front steps. Then I came back in and phoned Nancy. "Is Bo one of those women who . . . ?" I asked her. "Oh, no," Nancy says. "Well I don't want her here, anyway," I says, "not with my girls in the house."

After that I told my next door neighbour what had happened and she gave me a book on it.

PARTY

We were all over at Gracie's house. It was a Saturday afternoon. Everyone was in the living room drinking gin. This was Nancy's idea; she said she felt like a party. A drinking party on a Saturday afternoon! The sun was shining; Gracie's neighbours were out working in their gardens, kids were riding their bikes up and down the street. And I had a thousand other things I'd rather be doing at home: sewing, baking, planting Marigolds, you name it. But we were all there because Nancy wanted a party. And because she was a guest we had to do it.

There was Gracie and me (we were drinking tea), Arnie and Larry, and Nancy all dolled up like it was New Year's Eve (Billy was out on a boat). Bo was there, too, but I stayed away from her. And another woman, Hilda; I don't know where she come from. She was another one like Bo, very mannish. Man-haters we used to call them.

This Hilda was miserable. Never said two words all afternoon but sat on Gracie's chesterfield smoking Sportsman Plain and drinking one gin after another. Pretty soon Nancy's feeling good and starts playing the piano. She played jazzy tunes like "Kitten on the Keys", the sort of music you'd hear in honky tonks. And she was making up to Arnie that day which galled me, flirting with him, telling him he was a "real cutie". A cutie! Arnie was short and fat and bald, about as cute as a bed bug, but that day he was hanging over Nancy, grinning and slobbering, thinking himself Tyrone Power. It was then I suspected that

Nancy acted like this with all kinds of men but when I whispered as much to Gracie in the kitchen, she only shrugged. She just couldn't imagine anything bad about anyone. "Oh well," she'd say if she heard something nasty like a husband running off with a floozy. That afternoon she spent the whole time running back and forth between the kitchen and the living room serving ham and cheese sandwiches and pots of tea that no one drank besides her and me. Serving plates of store-bought cookies meaning it was a special occasion, too good for homemade.

But you know what drinking gin early in the day can lead to. Things started to heat up and it wasn't even three in the afternoon. There was Nancy at the piano laughing and carrying on, the belle of the ball, and Gracie and me sitting like two bumps on a log beside the fireplace, her in her apron, me in a house dress. And Nancy all swished up in a red crepe dress and those plastic shoes with the strap around the ankle. Come-get-me shoes we used to call them.

Bo was at the piano beside Nancy and the men singing "Oh Susannah" — I'll never forget that song. Hilda was by herself in the middle of the chesterfield smoking and drinking, getting madder by the minute. She had her legs crossed, the top leg was really swinging, back and forth, faster and faster, like she was winding herself up. Then she grabs one of the satin covered cushions off the chesterfield and starts punching it. Had it in her lap and she's hitting it with her fist. I could see Gracie getting worried because she was fond of that cushion; Larry had brought it home from the Korean War. It was done in cream satin and had a pagoda stitched in red and blue.

So we should have seen it coming. Hilda tosses the pillow to the floor. Then she grabs her glass of gin and throws it at Bo, at where she's standing with everyone around the piano. Gracie and me looked at one another. We couldn't believe it. Right there in her living room. The room that had the family pictures, the knitted slip covers on the arms of the chairs, and the Louis 16th clock, set up on the mantlepiece, brought by our mother all the way from the old country. A room as familiar as your own bedroom. It took a moment to sink in.

Finally Gracie says, "Oh heck!" and runs for a dish towel. The glass had landed on Bo's shoulder; it didn't cut her. But gin had spilled all over the back of Nancy's red crepe dress and she started to raise a terrible stink. Swearing, crying even about Hilda wrecking her dress. Didn't give a damn about the smashed glass or that Bo could have been hurt or about Gracie's ornament that broke when the glass hit it, a figurine of a girl holding a parasol, a Christmas present from my girls, I might add. Oh, no, Nancy didn't care two beans for any of that. Only about her dress.

Next thing Hilda starts to cry and gets up for the first time all afternoon. Goes over to where Gracie is sponging off Nancy's dress and throws herself at Nancy's feet. So dramatic. What's all this about? I was thinking. Never having seen anything like this before, not even in the pictures. But there she is, down on the ground hugging Nancy by the feet, hugging them plastic shoes with the red and black dice floating in the heels. "I'm sorry," she's crying, "say you'll forgive me."

Well, that put an end to the party. It was something the way it dissolved. Fifteen minutes haven't gone by when everyone goes. Arnie and Larry beat it to the basement and Hilda and Bo are out the door catching a bus. Nancy suddenly gets a headache and has to lie down. Grandma comes in from visiting the old lady across the street and sees me and Gracie still sitting on the kitchen chairs in the living room, stunned by what had just happened. "What's going on?" is all Grandma says, and then, still with her hat and coat on, starts clearing up the dishes. Pouring the half-filled glasses of gin down the kitchen sink.

But the problems between Nancy and Billy — I always figured it was because we had no money. That's what disappointed Nancy. She must have figured Billy's family was rich. We weren't. We were ordinary people. None of us had much of anything. Nancy must have took one look at the lot of us and felt sick. We must have seemed so dull. The way we shopped so careful, sewed our own clothes. The kind of life Nancy lived you read about in books: trips all over, wearing dress-up clothes every day.

Billy just went along with things, paying for everything, trying to please her; I guess he was hoping things would work out. But they didn't. As soon as winter came, Nancy got homesick.

"It's just a trip to see my mother," she told us again, using the same old story. But I knew it was a lie; I knew she wouldn't be back.

"She wanted to take the baby with her," Billy told me, "but I wouldn't let her." (He still called you "the baby" even though you were five years old.) He must have known Nancy was never coming back, too.

When you were three you called me Mommy but when you were five you wouldn't. And you never would. You always called me by my first name: Alice. Never Auntie Alice. Just Alice. It was like you were punishing me for something, though

I don't know what. You would have had a bad time living with your mother.

It didn't take me long to get you in shape after Nancy left, cleaned up and that, but I had a harder time getting you to mind. You were used to having your own way. One time you spit at me because I told you "No" and you had a lot of tantrums, especially at supper.

I've often wondered what those early years were for, those years I didn't have you. It would have been a lot easier if I'd kept you for good when you were three. Those years you had with your mother were a waste.

PICTURES

After a while we forgot about Nancy; we had our own lives to live. But she came up in conversation now and then. Usually about her clothes and how much fun she was at a party. But this was friends and neighbours talking, not family. They didn't know what she was really like: the trouble she caused at those parties making up to the men or that time with Bo and Hilda.

But she wasn't in our lives any more. We'd take pictures of you, though, and send them to her. Pictures of you in outfits I'd made: one in your skating dress when you started lessons, one in an Easter dress going to Sunday school.

But Billy wouldn't talk about her. When you started asking questions about Nancy I asked him what I should tell you. "Tell her nothing," he said, abrupt.

When you were eight or nine you got strange with Billy. We'd gone over to Vancouver to visit and you wouldn't have nothing to do with him. You were supposed to stay the night in his apartment while we went to a hotel but you wouldn't go. Screamed and carried on, clinging to me. I had to take you aside and tell you this: "Be good to your dad, you're all he's got." After that you stopped crying but you still wouldn't stay with him. I don't know what set you off. I said to Billy, "It's just a phase, ignore it." But he must have been hurt. You were everything to him.

All those years I had you, Billy spent his holidays with us, too. And when he retired he moved in with Arnie and me.

Nobody discussed it; it was just taken for granted that he'd live with us.

What he gave me for your room and board was fifty dollars a month. This amount never changed; he never gave me a raise. But he did pay for your lessons, dancing and piano. And he bought steaks for Saturday supper when he was over and later on a car that he left with me when he went back on Sunday nights. The other thing was every Christmas he gave me a hundred dollars in a Christmas card. The card would be waiting for me on the mantlepiece Christmas morning. I always acted surprised when I opened it.

TROUBLE

You thought nobody loved you. That was your problem. When you first came to me you'd wake up in the night crying and Arnie and me would take you in bed with us. Then you settled down and were okay to raise. Until you got to your teens. That's when you started asking questions. I was down on my hands and knees scrubbing the kitchen floor the first time you asked me plain: "Why did my mother leave me?" I couldn't answer because I didn't know. I could only say, "When two people stop loving one another" ... but I didn't know.

It made me mad the way Nancy never wrote to you regular. Now and then you'd get a letter but there was nothing in it — just Nancy telling about a trip she'd taken or later on, when she remarried, about her rich husband and their six Pekinese dogs. Birthdays were also hard on everyone. Because we'd never know if you'd hear from her. I think there were only two times presents actually arrived and then they were all wrong. One was a pair of black ballerina shoes three sizes too big. The other present I'll never forget; it came for your thirteenth birthday: a purple see-through nightie trimmed in black maribou and a pair of bikini underpants that said "Hi Sexy" on the bum.

So it's no wonder you got rebellious.

When you rebelled at going to Sunday school Billy said, "Let her sleep in." When you started wearing make-up to school he didn't bat an eye. Then Billy got you a dog, a white terrier, and you wouldn't look after him, you'd lock him in the furnace room and he'd dirty in there and you wouldn't clean it up. There was a lot of arguing and fighting. About the car when you got your licence, Billy's car that he left with me. Fights about staying out too late, once or twice all night. You'd smirk at me when I got mad; I could have slapped you. You'd do things to annoy me; it was the way you treated me, looked down on me as if I was your servant. My hands were tied a lot of times. Because you pitted me against your dad. And he'd always side with you. You'd tell him I was too strict, mean. I was helpless; I could never win against the two of you. Then when you were around seventeen I gave up; I left Arnie, I left you, and went to California, staying with a neighbour's sister. I was gone seven weeks. After a while you phoned me wanting to know when I was coming home. That surprised me; I didn't think you cared.

LOVE

*T*oo much gets said about love. Romantic love between men and women. The kind that goes on forever. The only place I've seen that sort of thing is in the movies or on TV. It doesn't exist anywhere else. Nancy and Billy are proof of that.

I got a fortune cookie once that said this: "Love is a few moments in the lives of lovers." I read it out loud to Arnie. A bunch of us were having supper at the Jade Palace. And Arnie said, "Now what the hell is *that* supposed to mean?"

He said it partly as a joke and partly because he didn't like the word "lovers"; he thought it meant something wrong like sneaking off and having an affair. But I knew what it meant: how with love the best you get is moments. The rest of the time you get worn down. Little things get said and these things become wounds that fester; you get put off. So after a while you'd rather keep company with women. And the men would sooner be with men. I think this is the way things are. It's too bad but what can you do? Before you know it a man has become another one of your kids. Someone to look after. I was always glad I had a sister. It must be a lonely life for a woman without a sister.

The last time I talked to Arnie about love was on Valentine's Day. Probably because it was in the air. The advertising. And in the stores, the chocolates for sale, the cards. Neither of us bothered with cards or presents; we hadn't for years.

We were sitting at the kitchen table having lunch, grilled cheese sandwiches. Rain was hitting hard against the window; the clouds were low down and moving fast. I shivered and said, "Miserable day," and Arnie said, "Mmmm." We never said much during lunch. I watched him eat his sandwich; he took little bites with his front teeth like a rabbit and, for some reason, this made me mad. When he was through I poured his tea and passed him the cookie plate. He didn't say thank you. He was staring out the window at the storm. I said, "Do you love me?" It just came out. The question hung in the air between us; I should have known better. He turned to look at me, startled, angry. "What are you talking about?" he said. Like I'd accused him of doing something wrong. I should have saved my breath.

So much for love. The other worry is sex. It's got nothing to do with love. It's something physical for men; they've got to have it. I often think of the pressure cooker I used for canning. Sex is like that for men; they need regular release. Or else the pressure builds up and they start to explode.

Arnie looked after the boilers at the library. Down in the basement. The heating system. I'd visit him there now and then when I went to town and we'd go for lunch, to Evelyn's Café next door. But he'd take me into his work room first where there were two huge boilers. And I'd watch him fiddle with the dials and knobs before we went out, everything careful measuring and worrying if things got too high on the dials or too low. I'd often think that's just how it is with us in bed, the timing, making sure he didn't go without. Arnie was proud of his work with the boilers. Just as I was proud of my work in bed.

But that was early on. Later things got different. We had a spare bedroom and Arnie started sleeping in there when he had a cold. And then he stayed. Said I snored and he could sleep better. "Me snore?" I said, "Try listening to yourself!" But any way you slice it, it suited us both. And I had the double bed to myself. I made a new quilt for it, done in pinks and greens and the shapes of flowers — a large flower in the centre offset by smaller flowers around the border. I got the pattern out of a book. It took me months to complete; much of it had to be sewn by hand, the pattern was intricate. I sewed many nights past midnight, my eyes getting so tired I could barely see. I had the sewing machine set up in my room, and the ironing board, everything I needed to work. Arnie would stick his head in every now and then to say I was missing something on TV. But I took no notice. I worked and worked. When the quilt was finally done and on the bed I just stood there and looked at it. I must have stood for an hour. It was so beautiful. My bed of roses.

*E*ach Sunday a roast of beef. For a change, chicken. In summer, ham and salad. Every week, year after year. You might find this boring. But I didn't. I liked it. Because having a plan meant I didn't have to think about food. This is a secret I never told before: I hated cooking. I hated worrying about what to put in everyone's mouths. This way I always knew what to cook. Mondays was leftovers. Tuesdays — soup made from the Sunday meal. (I always added a can of Campbell's Vegetable to the pot; no one knew this either.) Wednesdays was breaded veal cutlets. Thursdays — meatloaf. Fridays — fish. Saturday was broiled steak and pork and beans from a tin, summer or winter. If it was winter — on trays in front of the TV set for *Hockey Night in Canada*. Though I couldn't care less for the game.

I had other secrets, too.

Weekdays — always a nap after lunch. How else to get through the day? My greatest pleasure: to lie down and sleep in a clean house. When everyone was at work or school. Knowing that when I got up it would still be clean.

I enjoyed doing housework. I make no apology for this. There were days I'd as soon scrub a wall as do anything else. Vacuuming was another thing I liked. Because you got results quick. And I liked the way the carpet looked afterwards. Like a well-brushed dog. The way the nap stood out in squares of plush. Giving me a feeling of richness. I had a good vacuum cleaner, an Electrolux; it never gave me any trouble.

Dusting was good, too. You put a little perfume on your dust rag is what I did. Then everything smells sweet. A secret I learned from my mother-in-law. (The other thing she taught me was how to make creamed spinach on toast.) To get at cobwebs you put a tea towel over a broom.

About church, here's a secret: I kept my distance. I'd had enough church when I was a kid though I made you go to Sunday school just so you'd know what it was all about. But I couldn't see the sense of what they wanted me to believe. I've never had any attraction for God.

Cigarettes. Another secret. I liked the odd smoke. I kept two or three packs hidden in the freezer beneath the peas.

DEAD

Arnie's dying was a shock. He was sixty-four, still working at the library. Said he didn't feel well. For two days he missed work, wrapped himself in an afghan, sitting in front of the TV set. Said he couldn't get warm. I figured it was the flu. On the third morning I took him a cup of hot lemon. He was still in bed. It was my birthday, a bright March day. "Maybe you should go to the hospital," I said. Because he didn't look good. "All right," he says and starts to get out of bed. The next moment he was on the floor. I called the ambulance. They were here in five minutes. They said he was dead before he hit the ground. Heart attack. Billy was living with us then. I can still see him sitting in the easy chair by the living room window, stunned, crying. He couldn't get over what had happened. He drank half a bottle of rye before lunch.

After that Billy and me got an apartment in town. But I hated that apartment; it was cramped and dark inside, and in a busy section of Victoria with traffic going by day and night. I was glad when we moved to the Co-Op; it was more like a house and I could grow flowers around the back patio.

Billy died from our unit at the Co-Op. He started losing weight, getting thinner and thinner, and his skin didn't look good; it was grey in colour. And he had that look; I knew he wouldn't last long. He started waking in the night, not knowing where he was. Several times he fell; I couldn't lift him. Finally we got him to a doctor and he had X-rays taken. When he came home from hearing the results he looked upset. He told me they'd found two lumps in his chest. I nearly cried: two lumps, that's how he put it. When we knew it was lung cancer. Two lumps in his chest didn't sound as bad as tumours. He made it sound like two pimples. But that day he stopped smoking, threw his cigarettes in the garbage; he was seventy-five years old and he'd been smoking since he went on the ships at sixteen. I don't know what good he thought quitting would do him now.

I hated to see him put in the hospital but I couldn't look after him anymore. But you know all this. I was grateful when you took over. He was your father, after all, and it was your responsibility to see it through.

THE LOVELY HOME OF MRS. NANCY WICK

Those pictures Nancy sent you of herself in later years — I didn't recognize her. An old lady in a blonde wig. But even so she was still showing off what she had. In one picture she's sitting on the edge of her pool in Australia. You could tell the bathing suit was an expensive one. And the way she posed herself, flirty, an old woman acting the girl, that made me laugh. In another picture she's with a group of people sitting around a table drinking, a party of some sort, you can see the rings and the bracelets on her arms, the long dress she's wearing with the fancy embroidery. And Nancy smiling straight at the camera, the centre of attention, as if the picture was just of her.

Then there was the newspaper write-up she sent you. About her house in Surfer's Paradise. THE LOVELY HOME OF MRS. NANCY WICK the headline said. Taking up two pages in the paper. With pictures of the house on the water, of the lawns, and one of Nancy sitting on the living room couch holding a Pekinese dog. A LUCKY DOG it said under this picture. The dog I could recognize as a dog but I wouldn't have known Nancy, she'd put on so much weight.

The picture of her kitchen looked like something you'd see in a restaurant with two ovens and everything all shining counters (I knew she'd never set foot in there!). The article told about her flower garden, her brocade-covered furniture, the special run she had for her Pekinese dogs, six in all. There was even a picture of a baby grand piano and right away I could picture Nancy all dolled up and playing "Kitten on the Keys". So the newspaper write-up might have impressed some people. But not me.

When you told me she'd died I felt nothing. I almost said: "Tell me something interesting, something that's going to make me sit up and take notice." You said she was seventy-four but I wondered about that. Because she always lied about her age, putting it back five or ten years, whatever she felt like. When I first knew her she said she was twenty-six even though your birth certificate said thirty-one. The truth was probably closer to thirty-six. But it was hard to tell; she wore a lot of make-up, you never saw her unless she was fully made up. Otherwise she wouldn't show her face.

So seventy-four? Eighty-four? Who's to say? But she got what she wanted in the end: money. Marrying a rich man finally, one who owned hotels. Though he was sick with diabetes for most of their marriage and finally went blind. So she stuck with this man until he died and then got all his money. But it didn't do her any good because soon after she died herself — heart attack. So what use was all that money?

After Nancy died we found out she'd never divorced Billy but gone ahead and married any way. You weren't even mentioned on her death certificate; she didn't want any one to know you existed. That's when I put two and two together: Nancy was a bigamist. This explained everything. Why she had to keep quiet about you and Billy. Why she had to keep her marriage to Billy a secret.

WORRY

We all have our habits. I'd be the first to admit it. But you put up with differences. As long as they're not too bad. That is, if you want to stay in a family. Otherwise, off you go, out into the cold world, to find a home amongst strangers. But know this: the world doesn't care about you or your troubles. Your troubles are nothing, specks of dust; there's only your family. Be glad there's someone to worry over your daily scrapes. Be glad and thankful.

I wouldn't dream of changing a person. Deeply changing them. You can change some of the little things about them, the way they go about their business, their cleanliness habits, things like that. But you can't change their natures. Children are different, but not much. Different because you train them from the beginning, try to make them the way you want. But even children have their ways and won't always be bent; some are quiet and don't give their mothers trouble, some are a handful right from the start. The one thing children require is your time. I've proved that. With you who were so wild and spiteful. You took the most time of all. What was my secret? I kept you busy. Piano lessons, dancing lessons, badminton, skating. So you didn't have time to get into trouble. And I got Billy to pay for it. He could afford to. He made a good wage with no one else to spend it on. But it took a lot of my time, driving you places, sewing costumes. I don't think you realized the time I gave you. The years I spent worrying about you.

But what else is worth it? Nothing. There's not a thing that was more important than my children should be safe. As far as I'm concerned it's all births, deaths and funerals with a few weddings thrown in to keep things lively. The odd Christmas that stood out, the odd birthday. But mainly it's men and women getting through the years best they can. And disappointments. Many disappointments.

These were some of mine:

I wanted people to admire my house even though I was a janitor's wife.

I wanted a little trailer so I could travel the country but we never went anywhere.

I wanted enough money to always take care of my own.

I wanted many children but only had two. You were the third, a gift from my brother.

Navigation

OFFSHORE NAVIGATION

Night and the order is given. You take your place at the wheel and pull away from the dock. How well you steer the ship around obstacles, knowing just where to manoeuvre past the dim shapes ahead and beside us!

Standing sure on the bridge, feet apart, hands on the wheel, you're staring straight ahead. Your manner calm but your head awash with definitions: meridian, Rhumb Line, the Great Circle, the Equivalency of Time. And you're in command, you're at the controls. Guiding this cumbersome vessel, huge as an office building, unwieldy as a blimp.

It rains. There's wind. Soon a swelling sea. We ride the trough between the swells and each time we surface the engine shudders. It's good to nestle beneath the command of one so sure of his direction; I'm proud to stand beside you as your witness.

One by one the crew gets sick, fleeing below decks to lie down groaning, useless. But not us. Unaffected by the sea's rough course, we remain on the bridge, true sailors, riding out the storm.

Hours and hours you stand there steering. Glancing at the compass, peering through the rain-splattered window. You're pulling the ship along the imaginary path you worked out earlier, when the sun and moon showed which angles to use. You said there were times as a sailor when you served in four hour shifts: four hours at the wheel, four hours in your cabin asleep. But there are no shifts now. Only hours and hours. Your hands gripping the wooden wheel. Your shoulder muscles knotting from the strain.

Each ship, you said, was like a live thing beneath your hands, a power so large, so prone to outside forces, that you could only revere it.

We ride the sea like confident breast strokers plunging into the waves, resurfacing for air. The long, long anchorage behind us. Our destination, to me, unclear. But the ship, she leaps! And I wouldn't leave you for worlds.

THE PLAN

*B*ecause Nancy left us for Australia, I was raised by your sister Alice and her husband Arnie. And because you worked on the ships out of Vancouver and they lived in Victoria, you could only visit every other weekend. This visiting routine started when I was five and continued for thirteen years.

Often your job required you to travel up the coast to supervise the loading of lumber — to Campbell River or Cowichan Bay. On the rare occasions when a ship docked at Ogden Point in Victoria, Alice would take me down for a visit. There would be the scary climb up the dangling metal and rope ladder to the ship's deck. The rusty stripes of water leaking from the ship's hull. On board the heavy smell of diesel fuel, the wet tinny decks, the enormous cargo holds. And you waiting to take us to your cabin where a steward had placed on a silver tray, a pot of coffee, cookies, and a glass of lemonade for me.

You were a small, slight man. I know this bothered you, to be so small. You rocked on your heels when you stood in groups; I thought this was to make yourself seem taller. You had none of the arrogance, though, that small men who are successful often have. We knew you as a quiet man, accommodating, almost shy; it was hard to imagine you commanding a ship. At home everyone called you Billy, a small boy's name.

During your weekend visits you slept on a cot in the basement. (In later years you shared twin beds with Arnie.) I'd make you Sunday morning bacon and eggs, even at six years old — the yolks broken, the bacon soft.

In Vancouver you lived in a series of small apartments, as tidy as any ship's cabin. You had no close friends, only the family, or so the story goes. But is this true? Was there only us? You rarely spoke of others. Only that man in your office who moved his family to Australia then regretted his decision. He hated the life there, you said, and despair and ruin followed. You often mentioned this story, but as a moral, as a lesson of what happens to those who dream of Australia. Did you worry about me wanting to live there? About my leaving you? You should have known: even as a young girl I'd been trained to spare you that.

Your weekend visits were an occasion, though. Saturday mornings we'd meet you at the C.P.R. boat. For a while you brought me gifts — a doll, a game of Snakes and Ladders — though Alice soon put a stop to that: *You'll only spoil her... She'll want to see you just for the presents.* But how I looked forward to your visits! Because all weekend you were mine; you were with me every moment. We'd go to the park, play games together. And through it all, you were smiling, attentive. Everything I did or said delighted you. My daily life was transformed. Like Christmas or birthdays, I lived flushed with excitement.

Although it wasn't always wonderful. I became older and resentful of the time you required. And Alice annoyed: *Your father sees so little of you... Your father will be so hurt.*

Because you were good to me. Wasn't it true? Didn't everyone say so? And what about *Never a harsh word crossing his lips.* Never scolding, nor raising your voice in anger. *Oh, you're the apple of your Daddy's eye.* And didn't you love me? When there was another, on the other side of the world, who didn't.

THE RHUMB LINE

About Nancy in Australia, no one spoke. At least not when you were around. You were always being spared the awful truths I'd hear from Alice or your other sister Gracie, tossed about openly, when you were away: *She broke his heart . . . Cared for no one but herself . . .*

So we were careful not to mention her name in your presence, not to break your heart again. As if mere words . . .

But from the things I heard I created the story of your union. The freighter Orongie (of which you were First Mate) travelling from Vancouver to New Zealand. Your shore leave there and meeting Nancy at a party in Auckland. Where she was dazzling, of course, in that harsh red-lipped way of women who are famous for breaking hearts. Playing the piano for a crowd of singing, cocktail drinking people. *Oh, she loved to be the centre of attention.* Her sequinned dress, her black hair cut short and styled in waves. Your marriage soon after in 1946.

And then my Australian birth and you receiving the news by cable — on a ship somewhere in the Pacific. The disastrous attempt after that to establish a household with her in Vancouver. The marriage over after five years. And then you settling into what I thought of as your real life, your quiet methodical years. Before and after Nancy.

For most of my childhood Alice told me: "If anyone asks where your mother is, tell them she's on a long trip." But what did you tell people who asked? My wife has gone away? My wife is dead? Or did they never ask? Were they, like your family, afraid to mention her, afraid to disturb what they thought of as your devastating pain? And because of this did you become, to the rest of the world, a man who must live with his eyes averted?

THE CIVIL DAY

I visited you in Vancouver once when I was eight years old. But not alone. The family always travelled in groups: if one was going, why not three or four, why not bring along Grandma who doesn't get out much, why not the widowed Gracie who'd enjoy the trip?

Your apartment was a furnished bachelor suite on the ground floor of a large house off upper Granville Street. There were chestnut trees out front and a long shrub-lined driveway leading to the house.

You were waiting on the front steps for us — wearing your weekend clothes: grey slacks, a white shirt open at the neck, a light blue V-neck pullover sweater. And directing with your arm where Arnie should park the car. When this was done, you ushered us inside to the front lobby, all wood panelling and stained glass. When we entered the house Alice and Gracie lowered their voices and began whispering as if they were in church.

Inside the suite there was a neat single bed, a plush covered chesterfield, a small table for eating, and a kitchenette. Alice and Gracie wandered around the room, peering in the clothes closet, looking quickly out the tall windows then boldly went into the kitchenette and put on a kettle of water to boil. Gracie had brought homemade cookies, and Alice, a tin of sandwiches. Rummaging through the dishes they called out, "Billy, are these all the teacups you have?" and "Where's the sugar bowl?" "Where's the milk jug?" They were doing their preparation with their coats and hats on.

When tea was ready and everyone had a sandwich, we ate quickly, quietly. Grandma eating her lunch with her purse on her lap. You drinking your tea standing beside the window. The tea weak because Alice could never wait to pour it.

You had a radio set up on a dresser and a folding chair nearby so you could listen, you told us, to *Hockey Night in Canada*. This is where I headed as soon as I finished lunch, to switch it on, and be told, "Shush, not so loud." Then I went into your clothes closet which was large enough to walk around in. Beneath your suits covered in plastic from the dry cleaners, I found a large blue metal chest and opened it. Inside were souvenirs from the South Pacific: two carved wooden heads from Fiji, and woven mats and bowls smelling of vanilla. I found a pamphlet in handwriting — I recognized the writing as yours. Several pages long, it began: *My dearest darling Nancy* . . . But I quickly put it back, embarrassed by the emotion.

The visit was soon over. Alice and Gracie washing, drying, and replacing the dishes in minutes and telling everyone to use the bathroom before we left. Then the crowd of us squeezing into Arnie's Ford. You and me in the front seat with Arnie; you and Arnie taking so long looking at a map, figuring the best way to get to Stanley Park, that Alice in the back started banging on the seat behind Arnie's head: "For heaven's sake, get on with it." And then Alice, Gracie and Grandma giggling together and Alice, in a fake high-class voice, saying to Arnie, "Drive on chauffeur, I feel like a spin in the country."

THE DEFINITION OF TIME

*T*here was the summer trip we took to California when I was thirteen, catching the early ferry to Vancouver and picking you up on the other side. You swung what you called your "grip" — the same brown leather duffel bag you took to sea — into the trunk with the rest of the luggage and then climbed into the vacant passenger seat beside Arnie — the "navigator's chair" it was now called. Alice and Gracie sat in the back seat with me.

We drove down the coast through Washington and Oregon, to southern California, looping back through Nevada, Utah and Idaho. Driving four or five hundred miles a day and staying in small town motels because they were cheaper than in a city. Dinner was cooked in a motel that had a kitchenette. This is where Alice and Gracie prepared the next day's picnic lunch we would have, stopping along the road to eat it on a bit of grass or gravel so close to the highway we could feel the wind from the passing cars.

Entertainment in the motel rooms was TV and the novelty of different stations, different newscasters, different car lot ads. And clean sheets every night; this was the thing Alice and Gracie liked best, that and leaving dirty motel dishes in the sink. "We're paying for it," they'd say with a mixture of pride and guilt, "someone else can do the dishes for a change."

Sometimes the motel would have a heated pool and I'd be allowed to swim in it, the four adults watching me from side tables and sipping drinks of Orange Crush or Ginger Ale; no one drank. If it was very hot, you might dive in and swim a length. But always get out before I had a chance to splash you or play with you, towelling yourself off hurriedly and shaking your head violently to get the water out of your ears. You wore swimming trunks made of a blue Hawaiian print material.

The thing you got me to do on this trip was make a list of all the different licence plates I saw. Two columns — one for American cars, one for Canadian, with sub-headings under each column for States and Provinces. In the motel room at night you'd go over the day's tally with me. You'd do some figuring and then announce seriously to everyone: "Fifteen percent Canadian cars today, all from BC except two from Alberta."

The other thing you'd do was calculate the next day's route. From your "grip" you'd bring out a slide rule and compass ("The navigators tools," you told me), and with one leg kneeling on a chair would pour over the worn map of whichever state we were in. While I watched you figuring, Alice, Arnie and Gracie would be lying on top of their beds, shoes off, watching *The Mark of Zorro* or *The Lawrence Welk Show*.

The days were given up to driving. In the back seat between Alice and Gracie I'd often squirm. Sometimes it would be so hot in the car my bare legs would stick to the vinyl seat; I'd complain about the hot wind from the open windows or the length of the day's driving. Even though I was thirteen you'd turn around from the front seat and say, "Let's play I spy!" Or tell me jokes. You'd pat your bald head and say, "Think I'll get a hair cut. Matter of fact think I'll get them all cut." But mostly I stared out the window, past the dozing heads of Alice and Gracie to the empty landscape that we seemed always in such a hurry to drive through.

There were destinations to reach on this trip: The Trees of Mystery in northern California to see the redwoods and the giant statue of Paul Bunyan standing with an ax over his shoulder at the entrance to the trail; the "Eighth Wonder of the World", Grand Coulee Dam in eastern Washington where it was raining and we stood with the tour group watching foaming brown water pour into the river. The Golden Gate Bridge in San Francisco where, after the car had stopped at an intersection in the middle of the city, I proudly told everyone that I had stuck out my tongue at a black man and Alice slapped my arm and told me that was a terrible thing to do and you looked stunned and wouldn't talk to me for the rest of the day.

Alice and Gracie liked shopping in strange grocery stores during this trip, comparing prices, trying new brands. Any town we'd pass through, they'd both yell from the back seat: "Stop the car Arnie, there's a *Mr. Piggy*." And hurry off inside with you sounding worried, calling after them, "Don't be too long, we've still got two hundred miles to do."

If they were taking too long, I'd be sent to fetch them. Often I'd find them with hardly anything in their baskets. But standing together in front of an aisle of tinned fruit and vegetables marvelling at the variety, the cheapness. "At these prices, it doesn't pay to can them!" And then grabbing half a dozen tins of something (anything!), Alice would tell Gracie, "If Arnie starts beefing about fitting these things in with the luggage, he can just lump it."

And there was the day Alice and Gracie spent at the J.C. Penny store in Portland, Oregon, shopping for sheets and towels. The three of us wandered around the city to kill time and ate lunch at a cafe, sitting on swivel stools at a long counter.

The thing I liked best about eating in the States, I told you, was that you could have pancakes for lunch and no waitress would ever tell you this: "No, honey, that's just not possible."

You liked the coffee, you said, because in the States refills were free.

THE PLOTTING CHART

You kept a black, hard-back journal in which you recorded the cost of that summer trip. Columns were marked "$ for Gas", "Food", "Motels". At the end of the trip you added up the columns, calculating the total cost. In this way expenses were carefully shared.

This precision extended to the rest of the year as well; in another notebook you kept track of your savings plans — one for Christmas, one for the unspecified future which you called "Savings, General". Adding in the bank interest. Calculating what a year's bank interest would buy.

I imagined you ticking off my birthdays on a lifelong calendar. Entering my height and weight, childhood illnesses, in a special book. Noting the expense of me — how much for piano lessons, trips to the dentist. With a special column for the unexpected.

You bought a new suit every year. It went into first place in your closet, ahead of last year's suit, and the one before that. I imagined you flipping through these suits, marking the years, each year with its own colour, blend of fabric — navy, grey, brown, black, and the light-hearted year in the sixties when the colour was light blue and the pants had a bell-bottom flare.

There was a succession of new cars for Alice to use, as well. First a Zephyr, then two Fords, and then, while I was in High School, a pink Parisienne which I would often drive to school, or take my girlfriends in to drive around town on Friday nights.

Alice sewed most of my clothes — suits, skirts, coats in expensive fabrics; I picked the Vogue patterns. You bought jewellery for my birthdays — a black diamond ring, a pearl necklace, a dazzling broach with matching snap-on earrings made of turquoise and green glass.

As a teenager you liked me to dress up in the clothes and the jewellery and go for dinners with you to expensive restaurants leaving Alice at home. You *attended* me on these occasions — opening doors, helping me off with my coat. A fifteen year old in high heels and upswept hair, taller than you, and so embarrassed, afraid that people would not understand that I was your daughter. And that they should not pity us; you couldn't help this display, it was like an affliction, this need to show me off. You might have stood in the dining room of the Princess Mary Restaurant and cried to the room full of strangers: Look, here she is, my daughter. I believed we were *that* obvious. *That* exposed.

And so love enters the story again. And here is where I record how much it cost.

STEADY AS SHE GOES

When I passed the Grade 3 Royal Conservatory of Music Exam you gave me five dollars in a letter that began: Congratulations from Major C.

When I entered Junior High School you sent me another five dollars. This time the letter began: The Minister of Education is so pleased.

When I failed a Math test in Grade 11 you said, "Never mind, your fate is in the Arts." But two years later when I told you I wanted to be a writer, you said: You'll live a life of pain.

You also told me this:

Never buy a used car; you're only buying someone else's problem.

The knot you want when tying up a freighter is the bowline; it will never come undone.

Everything in the world is dynamic. Not static.

I need a hair cut. Matter of fact, think I'll get them all cut.

THE OBSERVED POSITION

Your last Vancouver apartment was on Cambie Street, a plain building across from a busy intersection. Because the traffic noise was loud you kept the curtain drawn day and night to muffle the sound. Inside the apartment it was stuffy, as well as being dark; heat came from a central furnace and there was no way you could turn it off.

During this time Alice showed you how to make beef stew: kidney, stew meat, onions, flour and water, baked for three hours. You would make this stew on a Saturday night and it would last you all week, eating it first with boiled potatoes and carrots and then, as the week wore on, with bread and butter.

In the evenings, if you weren't with a ship, you watched hockey or football on TV or played Solitaire at the kitchen counter. You said you often won. I wrote something at the time (I was eighteen) that began: The old man sits at the kitchen counter playing Solitaire snaps red queen on black king. And showed it to you. You asked if it was about you and I said no.

Later when I went to Europe, you pinned a map of the world across your kitchen cupboards. With red-tipped pins you marked the places I sent postcards and letters from — Montreal, St. Johns, Liverpool, Dover, Paris, Barcelona — and then carefully tied a thread between the markings to give a better idea of my route.

SIDEREAL TIME

*Y*ou took early retirement at sixty-two because, you said, you'd had enough. You said: "I don't care if I ever set foot on a boat again."

After years of living alone in Vancouver you returned to the Island, to the family. Sharing the same room with Arnie you'd shared on weekends for all those years. Sharing it full time now — twin beds with matching blue bedspreads. Alice having the big bedroom to herself. And when Arnie died, settling with her into a brother/sister union.

You bought a set of golf clubs but after a while gave it up because you had no one to play with.

You did your own laundry, made your own bed. Every morning a visit to Gracie's for the *Times-Colonist* crossword puzzle, then lunch. Then the drive home, the long afternoons. A book to read, a bill to pay, the hours spent at the kitchen table with pencil and paper calculating the household's electricity use, figuring out ways to save money. Saving money. You could make a razor blade last a month. Darned your own socks. Never called long distance. *If you save all your pennies you'll soon have a dollar.* The TV every night with Alice. Sitting in the easy chair with one foot curled beneath you. Your light blue wool socks.

The way you navigated your days.

TRUE BEARING

*S*o all these years, a careful dance you and I; our lives together, a kind of vacation. Where we did not mention faults or imperfections. Where you became a guest in my grown-up house, someone who minded his manners, didn't stay too long, didn't get involved. *Didn't rock the boat.*

And always the absence of Nancy. Where even mentioning her name in your presence was still imagined as a cruelty. As if your wounds, even after years and years, were still fresh, ready to bleed.

But I came to believe in your sorrow; it was more tangible to me than God.

What transpired? For me, growing up, the confusion of having two sets of parents, the divided loyalties: Alice and Arnie like understudies, deferring, retreating to the sidelines when you were around; and you, for the most part, as absent as Nancy, tucked away in your Vancouver life, there but not there.

So now I imagine your life. And this is a story about you and your voice is largely absent. And I realize with a shock that I seldom heard it; you died before I thought to listen. There are only phrases, remembered times, your imagined presence.

So love you? Oh, yes. Fiercely, and with devotion, protection. The way one loves the world, the sun, the sea, their children. The way we love anything we can't own.

THE GREAT CIRCLE

I was six months pregnant with my second child when you were diagnosed with lung cancer and went into the hospital. There were large tumors on each lung and, because of the advanced stage of the disease, an operation was out of the question. The doctor said maybe a couple of weeks, maybe a month. I was aware then of an annoying symmetry in the way events had unfolded; one in the family dying, one about to be born. But it was an arrangement, if you didn't exactly like, you would have found fitting. Because there was a design to it, a balance, a plus and minus, a static and a dynamic. Everything neat, orderly, arranged.

I tried to find beauty in your dying. The way you looked lying on the Emergency Room bed the night you were admitted. Calm. Your eyes so blue. The hospital gown, also blue. And hadn't your hair gone white? Sheet white? I hadn't noticed before; I'd always thought "grey". There was pink in your cheeks, too, and you were smiling, as if in amusement, humouring me, playing along. Putting up with the tests, the questions, for my sake. A game we were playing: *Pretend you are dying, no, pretend you have this awful disease and I'm the nurse come to make you well.* And you did look beautiful.

The seagulls on the ledge outside your hospital room. There was beauty in them, as well. The way they were always there, two or three of them, landing, flying by, sheltering from the February wind. More than anything, I wanted them to be your guardians, your escorts away from this life. "Look at the seagulls,"

I'd say to you. But seagulls had always been with you. All those years at sea. And you turned your head away from the window.

The first day in hospital you were full of energy and purpose — shaving at the small sink in your room, walking to the giftshop to buy a paper, a fudgsicle. Joking with the nurses, giving them your recipe for stew. *Oh, your dad's a real kidder!* Ordering a TV so you could watch the hockey games. Asking me to bring your book of crossword puzzles from home.

The next day this person was gone. Replaced by an old man tied in a chair, sedated, having trouble forming words. A stranger. What happened? The shock of seeing you like this, tiny, alone. They'd removed your teeth so you wouldn't choke on them. They told me it's not unusual in cases like this, the decline can be sudden. But I could see fear in your eyes.

A rapid decline. He's not in pain. It's just his breathing; he's having trouble getting air. Oxygen. The thin tubes, now, on either side of your nose. And the greyness everywhere: the colour of your skin, the light in the room. Outside the window as well, the dark grey clouds closing in. And the gulls on the window ledge squawking. I'd stand by the window looking out; it was possible to see the ocean off Dallas Road. Often it was stormy and the water looked angry and cold. Inside the room — the knocking of the ancient radiator, the stuffiness, the smell of disinfectant. The green bedspread pulled tight across your thin body. Your hands folded on your chest. The fingers, raw looking, swollen with arthritis.

To calm myself during the long daily drives to the hospital, I composed your obituary notice. Leaving out the date but mentioning relatives, mentioning Alice and how she'd cared for you at home. Noting your years at sea. And to whom you were beloved. I said: *He was a good man, a man you could count on.* Reciting the obituary to myself like a mantra.

The day before you died you tried to speak. Because of the tumors in your lungs, the supply of oxygen was not always reaching your brain. So that your words were unclear and you were having difficulty pronouncing them. But after several attempts I was able to understand this: You asked me, "Are you prepared?"

I must have looked confused because you got impatient then and waved your hand, angry. "Oh forget it," you seemed to be saying. Turning your head away.

Prepared for what? But then I understood. It was about charting my course. And did I have my maps in order, and did I know where I was heading?

You fix a point and move towards it. This is what you often said. My father, the navigator. Before you died you told me this: "One day I'll teach you to navigate by the stars."

THE CELESTIAL SPHERE

My father says: I learned to do everything at sea; through the years I did it all. I knew knots and painted decks, and as an officer I handled men. But what I liked best was navigation. The instruments, the calculations. I liked the accuracy and being sure. Before radar we used the stars. I knew every important star in both hemispheres; my calculations were never wrong. I navigated ships under sail and ships using steam and fuel. Through all kinds of seas and on both sides of the equator. I knew the currents in all the oceans. My speciality was manoeuvring around the obstacles — the sudden storms, the change of currents, engine problems, the deadlines for delivering cargo. I could read the sky, the wind, knew rain, clouds, fog, air pressure. I could tell what weather was coming by smelling the air. Even the ocean swells. Standing on deck at night, just by the roll of the ship, I could tell you how high, how fast they were running. All these things went into my navigation. It was more than numbers. It was my life. But it wasn't what I lived for.